The Missing Will
& OTHER STORIES

Agatha Christie

Pharos Books

ISBN: 978-93-55465-69-6
eISBN: 978-93-55465-75-7

©Publisher

Publisher: Pharos Books (P) Ltd.
Plot No.-55, Main Mother Dairy Road
Pandav Nagar, East Delhi-110092
Phone: 011-40395855, +4049916623
WhatsApp: +91 8368220032
E-mail: sales@pharosbooks.in
Website: www.pharosbooks.in
First Edition: 2023

Printed By: Sushma Book Binding House, Okhla
Industrial Area, Phase II, New Delhi-110020

The Missing Will & Other Stories
By Agatha Christie

CONTENTS

The Missing Will

The problem presented to us by Miss Violet Marsh made a rather pleasant change from our usual routine work. Poirot had received a brisk and businesslike note from the lady asking for an appointment, and he had replied, asking her to call upon him at eleven o'clock the following day.

She arrived punctually—a tall, handsome young woman, plainly but neatly dressed, with an assured and businesslike manner—clearly, a young woman who meant to get on in the world. I am not a great admirer of the so-called New Woman myself, and in spite of her good looks, I was not particularly prepossessed in her favor.

"My business is of a somewhat unusual nature, M. Poirot," she began, after she had accepted a chair. "I had better begin at the beginning and tell you the whole story."

"If you please, mademoiselle."

"I am an orphan. My father was one of two brothers, sons of a small yeoman farmer in Devonshire. The farm was a poor one, and the eldest brother, Andrew, emigrated to Australia, where he did very well indeed, and by means of successful speculation in land became a very rich man. The younger brother, Roger, my father, had no leanings toward the agricultural life. He managed to educate himself a little, and obtained a post as a clerk in a small firm. He married slightly above him; my mother was the daughter of a poor artist. My father died when I was six years old.

When I was fourteen, my mother followed him to the grave. My only living relation then was my Uncle Andrew, who had recently returned from Australia and bought a small place in his native county, Crabtree Manor. He was exceedingly kind to his brother's orphan child, took me to live with him, and treated me in every way as though I were his own daughter.

"Crabtree Manor," she pursued, "in spite of its name, is really only an old farmhouse. Farming was in my uncle's blood, and he was intensely interested in various modern farming experiments. Although kindness itself to me, he had certain peculiar and deeply rooted ideas as to the upbringing of women. Himself a man of little or no education, though possessing remarkable shrewdness, he placed little value on what he called 'book knowledge.' He was especially opposed to the education of women. In his opinion, girls should learn practical housework and dairy work, be useful about the home, and have as little to do with book-learning as possible. He proposed to bring me up on these lines, to my bitter disappointment.

"I rebelled frankly. I knew that I possessed a good brain, and had absolutely no talent for domestic duties. My uncle and I had many bitter arguments on the subject, for though much attached to each other, we were both self-willed. I was lucky enough to win a scholarship, and up to a certain point was successful in getting my own way. The crisis arose when I resolved to go to Girton. I had a little money of my own, left me by my mother, and I was quite determined to make the best use of the gifts God had given me. I had one long final argument with my uncle. He put the facts plainly before me. He had no other relations, and he had intended me to be his sole heiress. As I have told you, he was a very rich man. If I persisted in these 'newfangled notions' of mine, however, I need look for nothing from him. I remained polite, but firm. I should always be deeply attached to him, but I must lead my own life. We

                    The Missing Will & Other Stories

parted on that note. 'You fancy your brains, my girl,' were his last words. 'I've no book-learning, but for all that, I'll pit mine against yours any day. We'll see what we shall see.'

"That was nine years ago. I have stayed with him for a week-end occasionally, and our relations were perfectly amicable, though his views remained unaltered. He never referred to my having matriculated, nor to my B. Sc. For the last three years his health has been failing, and a month ago he died. I am now coming to the point of my visit. My uncle left a most extraordinary will. By its terms, Crabtree Manor and its contents are to be at my disposal for a year from his death—'during which time my clever niece may prove her wits,' the actual words run. At the end of that period, 'my wits having proved better than hers,' the house and all my uncle's large fortune pass to various charitable institutions."

"That is a little hard on you, mademoiselle," commented Poirot, "seeing that you were Mr. Marsh's only blood relation."

"I do not look on it in that way. Uncle Andrew warned me fairly, and I chose my own path. Since I would not fall in with his wishes, he was at perfect liberty to leave his money to whom he pleased."

"Was the will drawn up by a lawyer?"

"No; it was written on a printed will-form and witnessed by the man and his wife who lived in the house and looked after my uncle."

"There might be a possibility of upsetting such a will?"

"I would not even attempt to do such a thing."

"You regard it, then, as a sporting challenge on the part of your uncle?"

"That is exactly how I look upon it."

"It bears that interpretation, certainly," said Poirot thoughtfully. "Somewhere in this rambling old manor house your uncle has concealed either a sum of money in notes, or possibly a second will, and has given you a year in which to exercise your ingenuity to find it."

"Exactly, M. Poirot, and I am paying you the compliment of assuming that your ingenuity will be greater than mine."

"Eh, eh! But that is very charming of you. My gray cells are at your disposal. You have made no search yourself?"

"Only a cursory one, but I have too much respect for my uncle's undoubted abilities to fancy that the task will be an easy one."

"Have you the will, or a copy of it with you?"

Miss Marsh handed a document across the table. Poirot ran through it, nodding to himself.

"Made three years ago. Dated March 25, and the time is given also—eleven a. m.—that is very suggestive. It narrows the field of search. Assuredly it is another will we have to seek for. A will made even half an hour later would upset this. *Eh bien*, mademoiselle, it is a problem charming and ingenious that you have presented to me here. I shall have all the pleasure in the world in solving it for you. Granted that your uncle was a man of ability, his gray cells cannot have been of the quality of Hercule Poirot's!"

(Really, Poirot's vanity is blatant!)

"Fortunately, I have nothing of moment on hand at the minute. Hastings and I will go down to Crabtree Manor tonight. The man and wife who attended on your uncle are still there, I presume?"

"Yes, their name is Baker."

The following morning saw us started on the hunt proper. We had arrived late the night before. Mr. and Mrs. Baker, having received a telegram from Miss Marsh, were expecting us. They were a pleasant couple, the man gnarled and pink-cheeked like a shriveled pippin, and his wife a woman of vast proportions and true Devonshire calm.

Tired with our journey, including an eight-mile drive from the station, we had retired at once to bed after a supper of roast chicken, apple pie and Devonshire cream. We had now disposed of an excellent breakfast, and were sitting in a small paneled room which had been the late Mr. Marsh's study and living-room. A roll-top desk stuffed with papers, all neatly docketed, stood against the wall, and a big leather armchair showed plainly that it had been its owner's constant resting-place. A big chintz-covered settee ran along the opposite wall, and the deep low window-seats were covered with the same faded chintz of an old-fashioned pattern.

"*Eh bien, mon ami,*" said Poirot, lighting one of his tiny cigarettes, "we must map out our plan of campaign. Already I have made a rough survey of the house, but I am of opinion that any due will be found in this room. We shall have to go through the documents in the desk with meticulous care. Naturally I do not expect to find the will among them, but it is likely that some apparently innocent paper may conceal the clue to its hiding-place. But first we must have a little information. Ring the bell, I pray of you."

I did so. While we were waiting for it to be answered, Poirot walked up and down, looking about him approvingly.

"A man of method, this Mr. Marsh. See how neatly the packets of papers are docketed; and the key to each drawer has its ivory label— so has the key of the china-cabinet on the wall. And see with what precision the china within is arranged! It rejoices the heart. Nothing here offends the eye—"

He came to an abrupt pause, as his eye was caught by the key of the desk itself, to which a dirty envelope was affixed. Poirot frowned at it, and withdrew it from the lock. On it were scrawled the words "*Key of Roll-top Desk*" in a crabbed handwriting quite unlike the neat superscriptures on the other keys.

"An alien note," said Poirot, frowning. "I could swear that here we have no longer the personality of Mr. Marsh. But who else has been in the house? Only Miss Marsh; and she, if I mistake not, is also a young lady of method and order."

Baker came in answer to the bell.

"Will you fetch Madame your wife and answer a few questions?"

Baker departed, and in a few moments returned with Mrs. Baker, wiping her hands on her apron and beaming all over her face.

In a few clear words, Poirot set forth the object of his mission. The Bakers were immediately sympathetic.

"Us don't want to see Miss Violet done out of what's hers," declared the woman. "Cruel hard, 'twould be, for hospitals to get it all."

Poirot proceeded with his questions. Yes, Mr. and Mrs. Baker remembered perfectly witnessing the will. Baker had previously been sent into the neighboring town to get two printed will-forms.

"Two?" said Poirot sharply.

"Yes sir, for safety like, I suppose, in case he should spoil one—and sure enough, so he did do. Us had signed one—"

"What time of day was that?"

Baker scratched his head, but his wife was quicker.

"Why, to be sure, I'd just put the milk on for the cocoa at eleven. Don't ee remember? It had all boiled over on the stove when us got back to kitchen."

"And afterward?"

"'Twould be about an hour later. Us had to go in again. 'I've made a mistake,' says old Master, '—had to tear the whole thing up. I'll trouble you to sign again.' And us did. And afterward Master give us a tidy sum of money each. 'I've left you nothing in my will,' says he, 'but each year I live, you'll have this to be a nest-egg when I'm gone;' and sure enough, so he did."

Poirot reflected.

"After you had signed the second time, what did Mr. Marsh do? Do you know?"

"Went out to the village to pay tradesmen's books."

That did not seem very promising. Poirot tried another tack. He held out the key of the desk.

"Is that your master's writing?"

I may have imagined it, but I fancied that a moment or two elapsed before Baker replied: "Yes sir, it is."

"He's lying," I thought. "But why?"

"Has your master let the house? Have there been any strangers in it during the last three years?"

"No sir."

"No visitors?"

"Only Miss Violet."

"No strangers of any kind been inside this room?"

"No sir."

"You forget the workmen, Jim," his wife reminded him.

"Workmen?" Poirot wheeled round on her. "What workmen?"

The woman explained that about two years and a half ago workmen had been in the house to do certain repairs. She was quite vague as to what the repairs were. Her view seemed to be that the whole thing was a fad of her master's, and quite unnecessary. Part of the time the workmen had been in the study, but what they had done there she could not say, as her master had not let either of them into the room while the work was in progress. Unfortunately they could not remember the name of the firm employed, beyond the fact that it was a Plymouth one.

"We progress, Hastings," said Poirot, rubbing his hands, as the Bakers left the room. "Clearly he made a second will, and then had workmen from Plymouth in to make a suitable hiding-place. Instead of wasting time, taking up the floor and tapping the walls, we will go to Plymouth."

With a little trouble we were able to get the information we wanted. And after one or two essays, we found the firm employed by Mr. Marsh.

Their employees had all been with them many years, and it was easy to find the two men who had worked under Mr. Marsh's orders. They remembered the job perfectly. Among various other minor jobs, they had taken up one of the bricks of the old-fashioned fireplace, made a cavity beneath, and so cut the brick that it was impossible to see the joint. By pressing on the second brick from the end, the whole thing was raised. It had been quite a complicated piece of work, and the old gentleman had been very fussy about it. Our informant was a man called Coghan, a big, gaunt man with a grizzled mustache. He seemed an intelligent fellow.

We returned to Crabtree Manor in high spirits, and locking the study door, proceeded to put our newly acquired knowledge into effect. It was impossible to see any sign on the bricks, but when we pressed in the manner indicated, a deep cavity was at once disclosed.

Eagerly Poirot plunged in his hand. Suddenly his face fell from complacent elation to consternation. All he held was a charred fragment of stiff paper. But for it, the cavity was empty.

"*Sacré*," cried Poirot angrily. "Some one has been here before us!"

We examined the scrap of paper anxiously. Clearly it was a fragment of what we sought. A portion of Baker's signature remained, but no indication of what the terms of the will had been.

Poirot sat back on his heels.

"I understand it not," he growled. "Who destroyed this? And what was their object?"

"The Bakers?" I suggested.

"*Pourquoi?* Neither will makes any provision for them, and they are more likely to be kept on with Miss Marsh than if the place became the property of a hospital. How could it be to anyone's advantage to destroy the will? The hospitals benefit, yes; but one cannot suspect institutions!"

"Perhaps the old man changed his mind and destroyed it himself," I suggested.

Poirot rose to his feet, dusting his knees with his usual care.

"That may be," he admitted. "One of your more sensible observations, Hastings. Well, we can do no more here. We have done all that mortal man can do. We have successfully pitted our wits against the late Andrew Marsh, but unfortunately his niece is no better off for our success."

By driving to the station at once, we were just able to catch a train to London, though not the principal express. Poirot was sad and dissatisfied. For my part, I was tired and dozed in a corner. Suddenly, as we were just moving out of Taunton, Poirot uttered a piercing squeal.

"*Vite*, Hastings! Awake and jump. But jump, I say!"

Before I knew where I was, we were standing on the platform, bareheaded and minus our valises, while the train disappeared into the night. I was furious, but Poirot paid no attention.

"Imbecile that I have been!" he cried. "Triple imbecile! Not again will I vaunt my little gray cells!"

"That's a good job, at any rate," I said grumpily. "But what is this all about?"

As usual, when following out his own ideas, he paid absolutely no attention to me.

"The tradesmen's books, I have left them entirely out of account! Yes, but where? Where? Never mind, I cannot be mistaken. We must return at once."

Easier said than done. We managed to get a slow train to Exeter, and there Poirot hired a car. We arrived back at Crabtree Manor in the small hours of the morning. I pass over the bewilderment of the Bakers when we had at last aroused them. Paying no attention to anybody, Poirot strode at once to the study.

"I have been, not a triple imbecile, but thirty-six times one, my friend," he deigned to remark. "Now, behold!"

Going straight to the desk, he drew out the key, and detached the envelope from it. I stared at him stupidly. How could he possibly hope to find a big will-form in that tiny envelope? With great care he cut open the envelope, laying it out flat. Then he lighted the fire and held the plain inside surface of the envelope to the flame. In a few minutes faint characters began to appear.

"Look!" cried Poirot in triumph.

I looked. There were just a few lines of faint writing stating briefly that he left everything to his niece Violet Marsh. It was dated March 25, twelve-thirty p. m., and witnessed by Albert Pike, confectioner, and Jessie Pike, married woman.

"But is it legal?" I gasped.

"As far as I know, there is no law against writing your will in a blend of disappearing and sympathetic ink. The intention of the testator is clear, and the beneficiary is his only living relation. But the cleverness of him! He foresaw every step that a searcher would take, that I, miserable imbecile, took! He gets two will-forms, makes the servants sign twice, then sallies out with his will written on the inside of a dirty envelope, and a fountain pen containing his little ink-mixture. On some excuse he gets the confectioner and his wife to sign their names under his own signature; then he ties it to the key of his desk and chuckles to himself. If his niece sees through his little ruse, she will have justified her choice of life and elaborate education and be thoroughly welcome to his money."

"She didn't see through it, did she?" I said slowly. "It seems rather unfair. The old man really won."

"But no, Hastings! It is *your* wits that go astray. Miss Marsh proved the astuteness of her wits and the value of the higher education for women by at once putting the matter in *my* hands. Always employ the expert! She has amply proved her right to the money."

I wonder—I very much wonder what old Andrew Marsh would have thought!

The Adventure of the Egyptian Tomb

I have always considered that one of the most thrilling and dramatic of the many adventures I have shared with Poirot was that of our investigation into the strange series of deaths which followed upon the discovery and opening of the Tomb of King Men-her-Ra.

Hard upon the discovery of the Tomb of Tutankh-Amen by Lord Carnarvon, Sir John Willard and Mr. Bleibner of New York, pursuing their excavations not far from Cairo, in the vicinity of the Pyramids of Gizeh, came unexpectedly on a series of funeral chambers. The greatest interest was aroused by their discovery. The Tomb appeared to be that of King Men-her-Ra, one of those shadowy kings of the Eighth Dynasty, when the Old Kingdom was falling to decay. Little was known about this period, and the discoveries were fully reported in the newspapers.

An event soon occurred which took a profound hold on the public mind. Sir John Willard died quite suddenly of heart failure.

The more sensational newspapers immediately took the opportunity of reviving all the old superstitious stories connected with the ill luck of certain Egyptian treasures. The unlucky Mummy at the British Museum, that hoary old chestnut, was dragged out with fresh zest, was quietly denied by the Museum, but nevertheless enjoyed all its usual vogue.

A fortnight later Mr. Bleibner died of acute blood poisoning, and a few days afterwards a nephew of his shot himself in New York. The "Curse of Men-her-Ra" was the talk of the day, and the magic power of dead-and-gone Egypt was exalted to a fetish point.

It was then that Poirot received a brief note from Lady Willard, widow of the dead archaeologist, asking him to go and see her at her house in Kensington Square. I accompanied him.

Lady Willard was a tall, thin woman, dressed in deep mourning. Her haggard face bore eloquent testimony to her recent grief.

"It is kind of you to have come so promptly, Monsieur Poirot."

"I am at your service, Lady Willard. You wished to consult me?"

"You are, I am aware, a detective, but it is not only as a detective that I wish to consult you. You are a man of original views, I know, you have imagination, experience of the world; tell me, Monsieur Poirot, what are your views on the supernatural?"

Poirot hesitated for a moment before he replied. He seemed to be considering. Finally he said:

"Let us not misunderstand each other, Lady Willard. It is not a general question that you are asking me there. It has a personal application, has it not? You are referring obliquely to the death of your late husband?"

"That is so," she admitted.

"You want me to investigate the circumstances of his death?"

"I want you to ascertain for me exactly how much is newspaper chatter, and how much may be said to be founded on fact? Three deaths, Monsieur Poirot—each one explicable taken by itself, but taken together surely an almost unbelievable coincidence, and all within a month of the opening of the tomb! It may be mere superstition, it may be some potent curse from the past that operates in ways undreamed of by modern science. The fact remains—three deaths! And I am afraid, Monsieur Poirot, horribly afraid. It may not yet be the end."

"For whom do you fear?"

"For my son. When the news of my husband's death came I was ill. My son, who has just come down from Oxford, went out there. He brought the—the body home, but now he has gone out again, in spite of my prayers and entreaties. He is so fascinated by the work that he intends to take his father's place and carry on the system of excavations. You may think me a foolish, credulous woman, but, Monsieur Poirot, I am afraid. Supposing that the spirit of the dead King is not yet appeased? Perhaps to you I seem to be talking nonsense—"

"No, indeed, Lady Willard," said Poirot quickly. "I, too, believe in the force of superstition, one of the greatest forces the world has ever known."

I looked at him in surprise. I should never have credited Poirot with being superstitious. But the little man was obviously in earnest.

"What you really demand is that I shall protect your son? I will do my utmost to keep him from harm."

"Yes, in the ordinary way, but against an occult influence?"

"In volumes of the Middle Ages, Lady Willard, you will find many ways of counteracting black magic. Perhaps they knew more than we moderns with all our boasted science. Now let us come to facts, that I may have guidance. Your husband had always been a devoted Egyptologist, hadn't he?"

"Yes, from his youth upwards. He was one of the greatest living authorities upon the subject."

"But Mr. Bleibner, I understand, was more or less of an amateur?"

"Oh, quite. He was a very wealthy man who dabbled freely in any subject that happened to take his fancy. My husband managed to interest him in Egyptology, and it was his money that was so useful in financing the expedition."

"And the nephew? What do you know of his tastes? Was he with the party at all?"

"I do not think so. In fact I never knew of his existence till I read of his death in the paper. I do not think he and Mr. Bleibner can have been at all intimate. He never spoke of having any relations."

                    The Missing Will & Other Stories

"Who are the other members of the party?"

"Well, there's Dr. Tosswill, a minor official connected with the British Museum; Mr. Schneider of the Metropolitan Museum in New York; a young American secretary; Dr. Ames, who accompanies the expedition in his professional capacity; and Hassan, my husband's devoted native servant."

"Do you remember the name of the American secretary?"

"Harper, I think, but I cannot be sure. He had not been with Mr. Bleibner very long, I know. He was a very pleasant young fellow."

"Thank you, Lady Willard."

"If there is anything else—"

"For the moment, nothing. Leave it now in my hands, and be assured that I will do all that is humanly possible to protect your son."

They were not exactly reassuring words, and I observed Lady Willard wince as he uttered them. Yet, at the same time, the fact that he had not pooh-poohed her fears seemed in itself to be a relief to her.

For my part I had never before suspected that Poirot had so deep a vein of superstition in his nature. I tackled him on the subject as we went homewards. His manner was grave and earnest.

"But yes, Hastings. I believe in these things. You must not underrate the force of superstition."

"What are we going to do about it?"

"Toujours pratique, the good Hastings! Eh bien, to begin with we are going to cable to New York for fuller details of young Mr. Bleibner's death."

He duly sent off his cable. The reply was full and precise. Young Rupert Bleibner had been in low water for several years. He had been a beachcomber and a remittance man in several South Sea islands, but had returned to New York two years ago, where he had rapidly sunk lower and lower. The most significant thing, to my mind, was that he had recently managed to borrow enough money to take him to Egypt. "I've a good friend there I can borrow from," he had declared. Here, however, his plans had gone awry. He had returned to New York cursing his skinflint of an uncle who cared more for the bones of dead and gone kings than his own flesh and blood. It was during his sojourn in Egypt that the death of Sir John Willard had occurred. Rupert had plunged once more into his life of dissipation in New York, and then, without warning, he had committed suicide, leaving behind him a letter which contained some curious phrases. It seemed written in a sudden fit of remorse. He referred to himself as a leper and an outcast, and the letter ended by declaring that such as he were better dead.

A shadowy theory leapt into my brain. I had never really believed in the vengeance of a long dead Egyptian king. I saw here a more modern crime. Supposing this young man had decided to do away with his uncle—preferably by poison. By mistake, Sir John Willard receives the fatal dose. The young man returns to New York, haunted by his crime. The news of his uncle's death reaches him. He realizes how unnecessary his crime has been, and stricken with remorse takes his own life.

I outlined my solution to Poirot. He was interested.

"It is ingenious what you have thought of there—decidedly it is ingenious. It may even be true. But you leave out of count the fatal influence of the Tomb."

I shrugged my shoulders.

"You still think that has something to do with it?"

"So much so, mon ami, that we start for Egypt tomorrow."

"What?" I cried, astonished.

"I have said it." An expression of conscious heroism spread over Poirot's face. Then he groaned. "But oh," he lamented, "the sea! The hateful sea!"

II

It was a week later. Beneath our feet was the golden sand of the desert. The hot sun poured down overhead. Poirot, the picture of misery, wilted by my side. The little man was not a good traveller. Our four days' voyage from Marseilles had been one long agony to him. He had landed at Alexandria the wraith of his former self, even his usual neatness had deserted him. We had arrived in Cairo and had driven out at once to the Mena House Hotel, right in the shadow of the Pyramids.

The charm of Egypt had laid hold of me. Not so Poirot. Dressed precisely the same as in London, he carried a small clothes brush in his pocket and waged an unceasing war on the dust which accumulated on his dark apparel.

"And my boots," he wailed. "Regard them, Hastings. My boots, of the neat patent leather, usually so smart and shining. See, the sand is inside them, which is painful, and outside them, which outrages the eyesight. Also the heat, it causes my moustaches to become limp—but limp!"

"Look at the Sphinx," I urged. "Even I can feel the mystery and the charm it exhales."

Poirot looked at it discontentedly.

"It has not the air happy," he declared. "How could it, half-buried in sand in that untidy fashion. Ah, this cursed sand!"

"Come, now, there's a lot of sand in Belgium," I reminded him, mindful of a holiday spent at Knocke-sur-mer in the midst of "Les dunes impeccables" as the guidebook had phrased it.

"Not in Brussels," declared Poirot. He gazed at the Pyramids thoughtfully. "It is true that they, at least, are of a shape solid and geometrical, but their surface is of an unevenness most unpleasing. And the palm trees I like them not. Not even do they plant them in rows!"

I cut short his lamentations, by suggesting that we should start for the camp. We were to ride there on camels, and the beasts were patiently kneeling, waiting for us to mount, in charge of several picturesque boys headed by a voluble dragoman.

I pass over the spectacle of Poirot on a camel. He started by groans and lamentations and ended by shrieks, gesticulations and invocations to the Virgin Mary and every Saint in the calendar. In the end, he descended ignominiously and finished the journey on a diminutive donkey. I must admit that a trotting camel is no joke for the amateur. I was stiff for several days.

At last we neared the scene of the excavations. A sunburnt man with a grey beard, in white clothes and wearing a helmet, came to meet us.

"Monsieur Poirot and Captain Hastings? We received your cable. I'm sorry that there was no one to meet you in Cairo. An unforeseen event occurred which completely disorganized our plans."

Poirot paled. His hand, which had stolen to his clothes brush, stayed its course.

"Not another death?" he breathed.

"Yes."

"Sir Guy Willard?" I cried.

"No, Captain Hastings. My American colleague, Mr. Schneider."

"And the cause?" demanded Poirot.

"Tetanus."

I blanched. All around me I seemed to feel an atmosphere of evil, subtle and menacing. A horrible thought flashed across me. Supposing I were next?

"Mon Dieu," said Poirot, in a very low voice, "I do not understand this. It is horrible. Tell me, monsieur, there is no doubt that it was tetanus?"

"I believe not. But Dr. Ames will tell you more than I can do."

"Ah, of course, you are not the doctor."

"My name is Tosswill."

This, then, was the British expert described by Lady Willard as being a minor official at the British Museum. There was something at once grave and steadfast about him that took my fancy.

"If you will come with me," continued Dr. Tosswill. "I will take you to Sir Guy Willard. He was most anxious to be informed as soon as you should arrive."

We were taken across the camp to a large tent. Dr. Tosswill lifted up the flap and we entered. Three men were sitting inside.

"Monsieur Poirot and Captain Hastings have arrived, Sir Guy," said Tosswill.

The youngest of the three men jumped up and came forward to greet us. There was a certain impulsiveness in his manner which reminded me of his mother. He was not nearly so sunburnt as the others, and that fact, coupled with a certain haggardness round the eyes, made him look older than his twenty-two years. He was clearly endeavouring to bear up under a severe mental strain.

He introduced his two companions, Dr. Ames, a capable-looking man of thirty-odd, with a touch of greying hair at the temples, and Mr. Harper, the secretary, a pleasant lean young man wearing the national insignia of horn-rimmed spectacles.

After a few minutes' desultory conversation the latter went out, and Dr. Tosswill followed him. We were left alone with Sir Guy and Dr. Ames.

"Please ask any questions you want to ask, Monsieur Poirot," said Willard. "We are utterly dumbfounded at this strange series of disasters, but it isn't—it can't be, anything but coincidence."

There was a nervousness about his manner which rather belied the words. I saw that Poirot was studying him keenly.

"Your heart is really in this work, Sir Guy?"

"Rather. No matter what happens, or what comes of it, the work is going on. Make up your mind to that."

Poirot wheeled round on the other.

"What have you to say to that, monsieur le docteur?"

"Well," drawled the doctor, "I'm not for quitting myself."

Poirot made one of those expressive grimaces of his.

"Then, évidemment, we must find out just how we stand. When did Mr. Schneider's death take place?"

"Three days ago."

"You are sure it was tetanus?"

"Dead sure."

"It couldn't have been a case of strychnine poisoning, for instance?"

"No, Monsieur Poirot, I see what you are getting at. But it was a clear case of tetanus."

"Did you not inject antiserum?"

"Certainly we did," said the doctor dryly. "Every conceivable thing that could be done was tried."

"Had you the antiserum with you?"

"No. We procured it from Cairo."

"Have there been any other cases of tetanus in the camp?"

"No, not one."

"Are you certain that the death of Mr. Bleibner was not due to tetanus?"

"Absolutely plumb certain. He had a scratch upon his thumb which became poisoned, and septicaemia set in. It sounds pretty much the same to a layman, I dare say, but the two things are entirely different."

"Then we have four deaths—all totally dissimilar, one heart failure, one blood poisoning, one suicide and one tetanus."

"Exactly, Monsieur Poirot."

"Are you certain that there is nothing which might link the four together?"

"I don't quite understand you?"

"I will put it plainly. Was any act committed by those four men which might seem to denote disrespect to the spirit of Men-her-Ra?"

The doctor gazed at Poirot in astonishment.

"You're talking through your hat, Monsieur Poirot. Surely you've not been guyed into believing all that fool talk?"

"Absolute nonsense," muttered Willard angrily.

Poirot remained placidly immovable, blinking a little out of his green cat's eyes.

"So you do not believe it, monsieur le docteur?"

"No, sir, I do not," declared the doctor emphatically. "I am a scientific man, and I believe only what science teaches."

"Was there no science then in Ancient Egypt?" asked Poirot softly. He did not wait for a reply, and indeed Dr. Ames seemed rather at a loss for the moment. "No, no, do not answer me, but tell me this. What do the native workmen think?"

"I guess," said Dr. Ames, "that, where white folk lose their heads, natives aren't going to be far behind. I'll admit that they're getting what you might call scared—but they've no cause to be."

"I wonder," said Poirot noncommittally.

Sir Guy leant forward.

"Surely," he cried incredulously, "you cannot believe in—oh, but the thing's absurd! You can know nothing of Ancient Egypt if you think that."

For answer Poirot produced a little book from his pocket—an ancient tattered volume. As he held it out I saw its title, The Magic of the Egyptians and Chaldeans. Then, wheeling round, he strode out of the tent. The doctor stared at me.

"What is his little idea?"

The phrase, so familiar on Poirot's lips, made me smile as it came from another.

"I don't know exactly," I confessed. "He's got some plan of exorcizing the evil spirits, I believe."

I went in search of Poirot, and found him talking to the lean-faced young man who had been the late Mr. Bleibner's secretary.

"No," Mr. Harper was saying, "I've only been six months with the expedition. Yes, I knew Mr. Bleibner's affairs pretty well."

"Can you recount to me anything concerning his nephew?"

"He turned up here one day, not a bad-looking fellow. I'd never met him before, but some of the others had—Ames, I think, and Schneider. The old man wasn't at all pleased to see him. They were at it in no time, hammer and tongs. 'Not a cent,' the old man shouted. 'Not one cent now or when I'm dead. I intend to leave my money to the furtherance of my life's work. I've been talking it over with Mr. Schneider today.' And a bit more of the same. Young Bleibner lit out for Cairo right away."

"Was he in perfectly good health at the time?"

"The old man?"

"No, the young one."

"I believe he did mention there was something wrong with him. But it couldn't have been anything serious, or I should have remembered."

"One thing more, has Mr. Bleibner left a will?"

"So far as we know, he has not."

"Are you remaining with the expedition, Mr. Harper?"

"No, sir, I am not. I'm for New York as soon as I can square up things here. You may laugh if you like, but I'm not going to be this blasted Men-her-Ra's next victim. He'll get me if I stop here."

The young man wiped the perspiration from his brow.

Poirot turned away. Over his shoulder he said with a peculiar smile:

"Remember, he got one of his victims in New York."

"Oh, hell!" said Mr. Harper forcibly.

"That young man is nervous," said Poirot thoughtfully. "He is on the edge, but absolutely on the edge."

I glanced at Poirot curiously, but his enigmatical smile told me nothing. In company with Sir Guy Willard and Dr. Tosswill we were taken round the excavations. The principal finds had been removed to Cairo, but some of the tomb furniture was extremely interesting. The enthusiasm of the young baronet was obvious, but I fancied that I detected a shade of nervousness in his manner as though he could not quite escape from the feeling of menace in the air. As we entered the tent which had been assigned to us, for a wash before joining the evening meal, a tall dark figure in white robes stood aside to let us pass with a graceful gesture and a murmured greeting in Arabic. Poirot stopped.

"You are Hassan, the late Sir John Willard's servant?"

"I served my Lord Sir John, now I serve his son." He took a step nearer to us and lowered his voice. "You are a wise one, they say, learned in dealing with evil spirits. Let the young master depart from here. There is evil in the air around us."

And with an abrupt gesture, not waiting for a reply, he strode away.

"Evil in the air," muttered Poirot. "Yes, I feel it."

Our meal was hardly a cheerful one. The floor was left to Dr. Tosswill, who discoursed at length upon Egyptian antiquities. Just as we were preparing to retire to rest, Sir Guy caught Poirot by the arm and pointed. A shadowy figure was moving amidst the tents. It was no human one: I recognized distinctly the dog-headed figure I had seen carved on the walls of the tomb.

My blood froze at the sight.

"Mon Dieu!" murmured Poirot, crossing himself vigorously. "Anubis, the jackal-headed, the god of departing souls."

"Someone is hoaxing us," cried Dr. Tosswill, rising indignantly to his feet.

"It went into your tent, Harper," muttered Sir Guy, his face dreadfully pale.

"No," said Poirot, shaking his head, "into that of Dr. Ames."

The doctor stared at him incredulously; then, repeating Dr. Tosswill's words, he cried:

"Someone is hoaxing us. Come, we'll soon catch the fellow."

He dashed energetically in pursuit of the shadowy apparition. I followed him, but, search as we would, we could find no trace of any living soul having passed that way. We returned, somewhat disturbed in mind, to find Poirot taking energetic measures, in his own way, to ensure his personal safety. He was busily surrounding our tent with various diagrams and inscriptions which he was drawing in the sand. I recognized the five-pointed star or Pentagon many times repeated. As was his wont, Poirot was at the same time delivering an impromptu lecture on witchcraft and magic in general, White magic as opposed to Black, with various references to the Ka and the Book of the Dead thrown in.

It appeared to excite the liveliest contempt in Dr. Tosswill, who drew me aside, literally snorting with rage.

"Balderdash, sir," he exclaimed angrily. "Pure balderdash. The man's an imposter. He doesn't know the difference between the superstitions of the Middle Ages and the beliefs of Ancient Egypt. Never have I heard such a hotchpotch of ignorance and credulity."

I calmed the excited expert, and joined Poirot in the tent. My little friend was beaming cheerfully.

"We can now sleep in peace," he declared happily. "And I can do with some sleep. My head, it aches abominably. Ah, for a good tisane!"

As though in answer to prayer, the flap of the tent was lifted and Hassan appeared, bearing a steaming cup which he offered to Poirot. It proved to be camomile tea, a beverage of which he is inordinately fond. Having thanked Hassan and refused his offer of another cup for myself, we were left alone once more. I stood at the door of the tent some time after undressing, looking out over the desert.

"A wonderful place," I said aloud, "and a wonderful work. I can feel the fascination. This desert life, this probing into the heart of a vanished civilization. Surely, Poirot, you, too, must feel the charm?"

I got no answer, and I turned, a little annoyed. My annoyance was quickly changed to concern. Poirot was lying back across the rude couch, his face horribly convulsed. Beside him was the empty cup. I rushed to his side, then dashed out and across the camp to Dr. Ames's tent.

"Dr. Ames!" I cried. "Come at once."

"What's the matter?" said the doctor, appearing in pyjamas.

"My friend. He's ill. Dying. The camomile tea. Don't let Hassan leave the camp."

Like a flash the doctor ran to our tent. Poirot was lying as I left him.

"Extraordinary," cried Ames. "Looks like a seizure—or—what did you say about something he drank?" He picked up the empty cup.

"Only I did not drink it!" said a placid voice.

We turned in amazement. Poirot was sitting up on the bed. He was smiling.

"No," he said gently. "I did not drink it. While my good friend Hastings was apostrophizing the night, I took the opportunity of pouring it, not down my throat, but into a little bottle. That little bottle will go to the analytical chemist. No"—as the doctor made a sudden movement—"as a sensible man, you will understand that violence will be of no avail. During Hastings' absence to fetch you, I have had time to put the bottle in safe keeping. Ah, quick, Hastings, hold him!"

I misunderstood Poirot's anxiety. Eager to save my friend, I flung myself in front of him. But the doctor's swift movement had another meaning. His hand went to his mouth, a smell of bitter almonds filled the air, and he swayed forward and fell.

"Another victim," said Poirot gravely, "but the last. Perhaps it is the best way. He has three deaths on his head."

"Dr. Ames?" I cried, stupefied. "But I thought you believed in some occult influence?"

"You misunderstood me, Hastings. What I meant was that I believe in the terrific force of superstition. Once get it firmly established that a series of deaths are supernatural, and you might almost stab a man in broad daylight, and it would still be put down to the curse, so strongly is the instinct of the supernatural implanted in the human race. I suspected from the first that a man was taking advantage of that instinct. The idea came to him, I imagine, with the death of Sir John Willard. A fury of superstition arose at once. As far as I could see, nobody could derive any particular profit from Sir John's death. Mr. Bleibner was a different case. He was a man of great wealth. The information I received from New York contained several suggestive points. To begin with, young Bleibner was reported to have said he had a good friend in Egypt from whom he could borrow. It was tacitly understood that he meant his uncle, but it seemed to me that in that case he would have said so outright. The words suggest some boon companion of his own. Another thing, he scraped up enough money to take him to Egypt, his uncle refused outright to advance him a penny, yet he was able to pay the return passage to New York. Someone must have lent him the money."

"All that was very thin," I objected.

"But there was more. Hastings, there occur often enough words spoken metaphorically which are taken literally. The opposite can happen too. In this case, words which were meant literally were taken

                              The Missing Will & Other Stories

metaphorically. Young Bleibner wrote plainly enough: 'I am a leper,' but nobody realized that he shot himself because he believed that he contracted the dread disease of leprosy."

"What?" I ejaculated.

"It was the clever invention of a diabolical mind. Young Bleibner was suffering from some minor skin trouble; he had lived in the South Sea Islands, where the disease is common enough. Ames was a former friend of his, and a well-known medical man, he would never dream of doubting his word. When I arrived here, my suspicions were divided between Harper and Dr. Ames, but I soon realized that only the doctor could have perpetrated and concealed the crimes, and I learn from Harper that he was previously acquainted with young Bleibner. Doubtless the latter at some time or another had made a will or had insured his life in favour of the doctor. The latter saw his chance of acquiring wealth. It was easy for him to inoculate Mr. Bleibner with the deadly germs. Then the nephew, overcome with despair at the dread news his friend had conveyed to him, shot himself. Mr. Bleibner, whatever his intentions, had made no will. His fortune would pass to his nephew and from him to the doctor."

"And Mr. Schneider?"

"We cannot be sure. He knew young Bleibner too, remember, and may have suspected something, or, again, the doctor may have thought that a further death motiveless and purposeless would strengthen the coils of superstition. Furthermore, I will tell you an interesting psychological fact, Hastings. A murderer has always a strong desire to repeat his successful crime, the performance of it grows upon him. Hence my fears for young Willard. The figure of Anubis you saw tonight was Hassan dressed up by my orders. I wanted to see if I could frighten the doctor. But it would take more than the supernatural to frighten him. I could see that he was not entirely taken in by my pretences of belief in the occult. The little comedy I played for him did not deceive him. I suspected that he would endeavour to make me the next victim. Ah, but in spite of la mer maudite, the heat abominable, and the annoyances of the sand, the little grey cells still functioned!"

Poirot proved to be perfectly right in his premises. Young Bleibner, some years ago, in a fit of drunken merriment, had made a jocular will, leaving "my cigarette case you admire so much and everything else of which I die possessed which will be principally debts to my good friend Robert Ames who once saved my life from drowning."

The case was hushed up as far as possible, and, to this day, people talk of the remarkable series of deaths in connection with the Tomb of Men-her-Ra as a triumphal proof of the vengeance of a bygone king upon the desecrators of his tomb—a belief which, as Poirot pointed out to me, is contrary to all Egyptian belief and thought.

The Veiled Lady

I had noticed that for some time Poirot had been growing increasingly dissatisfied and restless. We had had no interesting cases of late, nothing on which my little friend could exercise his keen wits and remarkable powers of deduction. This morning he flung down the newspaper with an impatient "Tchah!"—a favourite exclamation of his which sounded exactly like a cat sneezing.

"They fear me, Hastings; the criminals of your England they fear me! When the cat is there, the little mice, they come no more to the cheese!"

"I don't suppose the greater part of them even know of your existence," I said, laughing.

Poirot looked at me reproachfully. He always imagines that the whole world is thinking and talking of Hercule Poirot. He had certainly made a name for himself in London, but I could hardly believe that his existence struck terror into the criminal world.

"What about that daylight robbery of jewels in Bond Street the other day?" I asked.

"A neat coup," said Poirot approvingly, "though not in my line. Pas de finesse, seulement de l'audace! A man with a loaded cane smashes the plate-glass window of a jeweller's shop and grabs a number of precious stones. Worthy citizens immediately seize him; a policeman arrives. He is caught red-handed with the jewels on him.

He is marched off to the police, and then it is discovered that the stones are paste. He has passed the real ones to a confederate—one of the aforementioned worthy citizens. He will go to prison—true; but when he comes out, there will be a nice little fortune awaiting him. Yes, not badly imagined. But I could do better than that. Sometimes, Hastings, I regret that I am of such a moral disposition. To work against the law, it would be pleasing, for a change."

"Cheer up, Poirot; you know you are unique in your own line."

"But what is there on hand in my own line?"

I picked up the paper.

"Here's an Englishman mysteriously done to death in Holland," I said.

"They always say that—and later they find that he ate the tinned fish and that his death is perfectly natural."

"Well, if you're determined to grouse!"

"Tiens!" said Poirot, who had strolled across to the window. "Here in the street is what they call in novels a 'heavily veiled lady.' She mounts the steps; she rings the bell—she comes to consult us. Here is a possibility of something interesting. When one is as young and pretty as that one, one does not veil the face except for a big affair."

A minute later our visitor was ushered in. As Poirot had said, she was indeed heavily veiled. It was impossible to distinguish her features until she raised her veil of black Spanish lace. Then I saw that Poirot's intuition had been right; the lady was extremely pretty, with fair hair and blue eyes. From the costly simplicity of her attire, I deduced at once that she belonged to the upper strata of society.

"Monsieur Poirot," said the lady in a soft, musical voice, "I am in great trouble. I can hardly believe that you can help me, but I have heard such wonderful things of you that I come literally as the last hope to beg you to do the impossible."

"The impossible, it pleases me always," said Poirot. "Continue, I beg of you, mademoiselle."

Our fair guest hesitated.

"But you must be frank," added Poirot. "You must not leave me in the dark on any point."

"I will trust you," said the girl suddenly. "You have heard of Lady Millicent Castle Vaughan?"

I looked up with keen interest. The announcement of Lady Millicent's engagement to the young Duke of Southshire had appeared a few days previously. She was, I knew, the fifth daughter of an impecunious Irish peer, and the Duke of Southshire was one of the best matches in England.

"I am Lady Millicent," continued the girl. "You may have read of my engagement. I should be one of the happiest girls alive; but oh, M. Poirot, I am in terrible trouble! There is a man, a horrible man—his name is Lavington; and he—I hardly know how to tell you. There was a letter I wrote—I was only sixteen at the time; and he—he—"

"A letter that you wrote to this Mr. Lavington?"

"Oh no—not to him! To a young soldier—I was very fond of him— he was killed in the war."

"I understand," said Poirot kindly.

"It was a foolish letter, an indiscreet letter, but indeed, M. Poirot, nothing more. But there are phrases in it which—which might bear a different interpretation."

"I see," said Poirot. "And this letter has come into the possession of Mr. Lavington?"

"Yes, and he threatens, unless I pay him an enormous sum of money, a sum that is quite impossible for me to raise, to send it to the Duke."

"The dirty swine!" I ejaculated. "I beg your pardon, Lady Millicent."

"Would it not be wiser to confess all to your future husband?"

"I dare not, M. Poirot. The Duke is a rather peculiar character, jealous and suspicious and prone to believe the worst. I might as well break off my engagement at once."

"Dear, dear," said Poirot with an expressive grimace. "And what do you want me to do, milady?"

"I thought perhaps that I might ask Mr. Lavington to call upon you. I would tell him that you were empowered by me to discuss the matter. Perhaps you could reduce his demands."

"What sum does he mention?"

"Twenty thousand pounds—an impossibility. I doubt if I could raise a thousand, even."

"You might perhaps borrow the money on the prospect of your approaching marriage—but I doubt if you could get hold of half that sum. Besides—eh bien, it is repungnant to me that you should pay! No, the ingenuity of Hercule Poirot shall defeat your enemies! Send me this Mr. Lavington. Is he likely to bring the letter with him?"

The girl shook her head.

"I do not think so. He is very cautious."

"I suppose there is no doubt that he really has it?"

"He showed it to me when I went to his house."

"You went to his house? That was very imprudent, milady."

"Was it? I was so desperate. I hoped my entreaties might move him."

"Oh, là là! The Lavingtons of this world are not moved by entreaties! He would welcome them as showing how much importance you attached to the document. Where does he live, this fine gentleman?"

"At Buona Vista, Wimbledon. I went there after dark—" Poirot groaned. "I declared that I would inform the police in the end, but he only laughed in a horrid, sneering manner. 'By all means, my dear Lady Millicent, do so if you wish,' he said."

"Yes, it is hardly an affair for the police," murmured Poirot.

" 'But I think you will be wiser than that,' he continued. 'See, here is your letter—in this little Chinese puzzle box!' He held it so that I could see. I tried to snatch at it, but he was too quick for me. With a horrid smile he folded it up and replaced it in the little wooden box. 'It will be quite safe here, I assure you,' he said, 'and the box itself lives in such a clever place that you would never find it.' My eyes turned to the small wall safe, and he shook his head and laughed. 'I have a better safe than that,' he said. Oh, he was odious! M. Poirot, do you think that you can help me?"

"Have faith in Papa Poirot. I will find a way."

These reassurances were all very well, I thought, as Poirot gallantly ushered his fair client down the stairs, but it seemed to me that we had a tough nut to crack. I said as much to Poirot when he returned. He nodded ruefully.

"Yes—the solution does not leap to the eye. He has the whip hand, this M. Lavington. For the moment I do not see how we are to circumvent him."

II

Mr. Lavington duly called upon us that afternoon. Lady Millicent had spoken truly when she described him as an odious man. I felt a positive tingling in the end of my boot, so keen was I to kick him down the stairs. He was blustering and overbearing in manner, laughed Poirot's gentle suggestions to scorn, and generally showed himself as master of the situation. I could not help feeling that Poirot was hardly appearing at his best. He looked discouraged and crestfallen.

"Well, gentlemen," said Lavington, as he took up his hat, "we don't seem to be getting much further. The case stands like this: I'll let the Lady Millicent off cheap, as she is such a charming young lady." He leered odiously. "We'll say eighteen thousand. I'm off to Paris today—a little piece of business to attend to over there. I shall be back on

Tuesday. Unless the money is paid by Tuesday evening, the letter goes to the Duke. Don't tell me Lady Millicent can't raise the money. Some of her gentlemen friends would be only too willing to oblige such a pretty woman with a loan—if she goes the right way about it."

My face flushed, and I took a step forward, but Lavington had wheeled out of the room as he finished his sentence.

"My God!" I cried. "Something has got to be done. You seem to be taking this lying down, Poirot."

"You have an excellent heart, my friend—but your grey cells are in a deplorable condition. I have no wish to impress Mr. Lavington with my capabilities. The more pusillanimous he thinks me, the better."

"Why?"

"It is curious," murmured Poirot reminiscently, "that I should have uttered a wish to work against the law just before Lady Millicent arrived!"

"You are going to burgle his house while he is away?" I gasped.

"Sometimes, Hastings, your mental processes are amazingly quick."

"Suppose he takes the letter with him?"

Poirot shook his head.

"That is very unlikely. He has evidently a hiding place in his house that he fancies to be pretty impregnable."

"When do we—er—do the deed?"

"Tomorrow night. We will start from here about eleven o'clock."

III

At the time appointed I was ready to set off. I had donned a dark suit, and a soft dark hat. Poirot beamed kindly on me.

"You have dressed the part, I see," he observed. "Come let us take the underground to Wimbledon."

"Aren't we going to take anything with us? Tools to break in with?"

"My dear Hastings, Hercule Poirot does not adopt such crude methods."

I retired, snubbed, but my curiosity was alert.

It was just on midnight that we entered the small suburban garden of Buona Vista. The house was dark and silent. Poirot went straight to a window at the back of the house, raised the sash noiselessly and bade me enter.

"How did you know this window would be open?" I whispered, for really it seemed uncanny.

"Because I sawed through the catch this morning."

"What?"

"But yes, it was most simple. I called, presented a fictitious card and one of Inspector Japp's official ones. I said I had been sent, recommended by Scotland Yard, to attend to some burglar-proof fastenings that Mr. Lavington wanted fixed while he was away. The housekeeper welcomed me with enthusiasm. It seems they have had two attempted burglaries here lately—evidently our little idea has occurred to other clients of Mr. Lavington's—with nothing of value taken. I examined all the windows, made my little arrangement, forbade the servants to touch the windows until tomorrow, as they were electrically connected up, and withdrew gracefully."

"Really, Poirot, you are wonderful."

"Mon ami, it was of the simplest. Now, to work! The servants sleep at the top of the house, so we will run little risk of disturbing them."

"I presume the safe is built into the wall somewhere?"

"Safe? Fiddlesticks! There is no safe. Mr. Lavington is an intelligent man. You will see, he will have devised a hiding place much more intelligent than a safe. A safe is the first thing everyone looks for."

Whereupon we began a systematic search of the entire place. But after several hours ransacking the house, our search had been unavailing. I saw symptoms of anger gathering on Poirot's face.

"Ah, sapristi, is Hercule Poirot to be beaten? Never! Let us be calm. Let us reflect. Let us reason. Let us—enfin!—employ our little grey cells!"

He paused for some moments, bending his brows in concentration; then the green light I knew so well stole into his eyes.

"I have been an imbecile! The kitchen!"

"The kitchen," I cried. "But that's impossible. The servants!"

"Exactly. Just what ninety-nine people out of a hundred would say! And for that very reason the kitchen is the ideal place to choose. It is full of various homely objects. En avant, to the kitchen!"

I followed him, completely sceptical, and watched whilst he dived into bread bins, tapped saucepans, and put his head into the gas oven. In the end, tired of watching him, I strolled back to the study. I was convinced that there, and there only, would we find the cache. I made a further minute search, noted that it was now a quarter past four and that therefore it would soon be growing light, and then went back to the kitchen regions.

To my utter amazement, Poirot was now standing right inside the coal bin, to the utter ruin of his neat light suit. He made a grimace.

"But yes, my friend, it is against all my instincts so to ruin my appearance, but what will you?"

"But Lavington can't have buried it under the coal?"

"If you would use your eyes, you would see that it is not the coal that I examine."

I then saw on a shelf behind the coal bunker some logs of wood were piled. Poirot was dexterously taking them down one by one. Suddenly he uttered a low exclamation.

"Your knife, Hastings!"

I handed it to him. He appeared to inset it in the wood, and suddenly the log split in two. It had been neatly sawn in half and a cavity hollowed out in the centre. From this cavity Poirot took a little wooden box of Chinese make.

"Well done!" I cried, carried out of myself.

"Gently, Hastings! Do not raise your voice too much. Come, let us be off, before the daylight is upon us."

Slipping the box into his pocket, he leaped lightly out of the coal-bunker, brushed himself down as well as he could, and leaving the house by the same way as we had come, we walked rapidly in the direction of London.

"But what an extraordinary place!" I expostulated. "Anyone might have used the log."

"In July, Hastings? And it was at the bottom of the pile—a very ingenious hiding place. Ah, here is a taxi! Now for home, a wash, and a refreshing sleep."

IV

After the excitement of the night, I slept late. When I finally strolled into our sitting room just before one o'clock, I was surprised to see Poirot, leaning back in an armchair, the Chinese box open beside him, calmly reading the letter he had taken from it.

He smiled at me affectionately, and tapped the sheet he held.

"She was right, the Lady Millicent; never would the Duke have pardoned this letter! It contains some of the most extravagant terms of affection I have ever come across."

"Really, Poirot," I said, rather disgustedly, "I don't think you should have read the letter. "That's the sort of thing that isn't done."

"It is done by Hercule Poirot," replied my friend imperturbably.

"And another thing," I said. "I don't think using Japp's official card yesterday was quite playing the game."

"But I was not playing a game, Hastings. I was conducting a case."

I shrugged my shoulders. One can't argue with a point of view.

"A step on the stairs," said Poirot. "That will be Lady Millicent."

Our fair client came in with an anxious expression on her face which changed to one of delight on seeing the letter and box which Poirot held up.

"Oh, M. Poirot. How wonderful of you! How did you do it?"

"By rather reprehensible methods, milady. But Mr. Lavington will not prosecute. This is your letter, is it not?"

She glanced through it.

"Yes. Oh, how can I ever thank you! You are a wonderful, wonderful man. Where was it hidden?"

Poirot told her.

"How very clever of you!" She took up the small box from the table. "I shall keep this as a souvenir."

"I had hoped, milady, that you would permit me to keep it—also as a souvenir."

"I hope to send you a better souvenir than that—on my wedding day. You shall not find me ungrateful, M. Poirot."

"The pleasure of doing you a service will be more to me than a cheque—so you permit that I retain the box."

"Oh no, M. Poirot, I simply must have that," she cried laughingly.

She stretched out her hand, but Poirot was before her. His hand closed over it.

"I think not." His voice had changed.

"What do you mean?" Her voice seemed to have grown sharper.

"At any rate, permit me to abstract its further contents. You observed that the original cavity has been reduced by half. In the top half, the compromising letter; in the bottom—"

He made a nimble gesture, then held out his hand. On the palm were four large glittering stones, and two big milky white pearls.

"The jewels stolen in Bond Street the other day, I rather fancy," murmured Poirot. "Japp will tell us."

To my utter amazement, Japp himself stepped out from Poirot's bedroom.

"An old friend of yours, I believe," said Poirot politely to Lady Millicent.

"Nabbed, by the Lord!" said Lady Millicent, with a complete change of manner. "You nippy old devil!" She looked at Poirot with almost affectionate awe.

"Well, Gertie, my dear," said Japp, "the game's up this time, I fancy. Fancy seeing you again so soon! We've got your pal, too, the gentleman who called here the other day calling himself Lavington. As for Lavington himself, alias Croker, alias Reed, I wonder which of the gang it was who stuck a knife into him the other day in Holland? Thought he'd got the goods with him, didn't you? And he hadn't. He double-crossed you properly—hid 'em in his own house. You had two fellows looking for them, and then you tackled M. Poirot here, and by a piece of amazing luck he found them."

"You do like talking, don't you?" said the late Lady Millicent. "Easy there, now. I'll go quietly. You can't say that I'm not the perfect lady. Ta-ta, all!"

"The shoes were wrong," said Poirot dreamily, while I was still too stupefied to speak. "I have made my little observations of your English nation, and a lady, a born lady, is always particular about her shoes. She may have shabby clothes, but she will be well shod. Now, this Lady Millicent had smart, expensive clothes, and cheap shoes. It was not likely that either you or I should have seen the real Lady Millicent; she has been very little in London, and this girl had a certain superficial resemblance which would pass well enough. As I say, the shoes first awakened my suspicions, and then her story— and her veil—were a little melodramatic, eh? The Chinese box with a bogus compromising letter in the top must have been known to all the gang, but the log of wood was the late Mr. Lavington's idea. Eh, par example, Hastings, I hope you will not again wound my feelings as you did yesterday by saying that I am unknown to the criminal classes. Ma foi, they even employ me when they themselves fail!"

***

The Adventure of the Clapham Cook

I

At the time that I was sharing rooms with my friend Hercule Poirot, it was my custom to read aloud to him the headlines in the morning newspaper, the Daily Blare.

The Daily Blare was a paper that made the most of any opportunity for sensationalism. Robberies and murders did not lurk obscurely in its back pages. Instead they hit you in the eye in large type on the front page.

ABSCONDING BANK CLERK DISAPPEARS WITH FIFTY THOUSAND POUNDS' WORTH OF NEGOTIABLE SECURITIES, I read.

HUSBAND PUTS HIS HEAD IN GAS-OVEN. UNHAPPY HOME LIFE. MISSING TYPIST. PRETTY GIRL OF TWENTY-ONE. WHERE IS EDNA FIELD?

"There you are, Poirot, plenty to choose from. An absconding bank clerk, a mysterious suicide, a missing typist—which will you have?"

My friend was in a placid mood. He quietly shook his head.

"I am not greatly attracted to any of them, mon ami. Today I feel inclined for the life of ease. It would have to be a very interesting problem to tempt me from my chair. See you, I have affairs of importance of my own to attend to."

"Such as?"

"My wardrobe, Hastings. If I mistake not, there is on my new grey suit the spot of grease—only the unique spot, but it is sufficient to trouble me. Then there is my winter overcoat—I must lay him aside in the powder of Keatings. And I think—yes, I think—the moment is ripe for the trimmings of my moustaches—and afterwards I must apply the pomade."

"Well," I said, strolling to the window, "I doubt if you'll be able to carry out this delirious programme. That was a ring at the bell. You have a client."

"Unless the affair is one of national importance, I touch it not," declared Poirot with dignity.

A moment later our privacy was invaded by a stout red-faced lady who panted audibly as a result of her rapid ascent of the stairs.

"You're M. Poirot?" she demanded, as she sank into a chair.

"I am Hercule Poirot, yes, madame."

"You're not a bit like what I thought you'd be," said the lady, eyeing him with some disfavour. "Did you pay for the bit in the paper saying what a clever detective you were, or did they put it in themselves?"

"Madame!" said Poirot, drawing himself up.

"I'm sorry, I'm sure, but you know what these papers are nowadays. You begin reading a nice article: 'What a bride said to her plain unmarried friend,' and it's all about a simple thing you buy at the chemist's and shampoo your hair with. Nothing but puff. But no offence taken, I hope? I'll tell you what I want you to do for me. I want you to find my cook."

Poirot stared at her; for once his ready tongue failed him. I turned aside to hide the broadening smile I could not control.

"It's all this wicked dole," continued the lady. "Putting ideas into servants' heads, wanting to be typists and what nots. Stop the dole, that's what I say. I'd like to know what my servants have to complain of—afternoon and evening off a week, alternate Sundays, washing put out, same food as we have—and never a bit of margarine in the house, nothing but the very best butter."

She paused for want of breath and Poirot seized his opportunity. He spoke in his haughtiest manner, rising to his feet as he did so.

"I fear you are making a mistake, madame. I am not holding an inquiry into the conditions of domestic service. I am a private detective."

"I know that," said our visitor. "Didn't I tell you I wanted you to find my cook for me? Walked out of the house on Wednesday, without so much as a word to me, and never came back."

"I am sorry, madame, but I do not touch this particular kind of business. I wish you good morning."

Our visitor snorted with indignation.

"That's it, is it, my fine fellow? Too proud, eh? Only deal with Government secrets and countesses' jewels? Let me tell you a servant's every bit as important as a tiara to a woman in my position. We can't all be fine ladies going out in our motors with our diamonds and our pearls. A good cook's a good cook—and when you lose her, it's as much to you as her pearls are to some fine lady."

For a moment or two it appeared to be a toss up between Poirot's dignity and his sense of humour. Finally he laughed and sat down again.

"Madame, you are in the right, and I am in the wrong. Your remarks are just and intelligent. This case will be a novelty. Never yet have I hunted a missing domestic. Truly here is the problem of national importance that I was demanding of fate just before your arrival. En avant! You say this jewel of a cook went out on Wednesday and did not return. That is the day before yesterday."

"Yes, it was her day out."

"But probably, madame, she has met with some accident. Have you inquired at any of the hospitals?"

    The Missing Will & Other Stories

"That's exactly what I thought yesterday, but this morning, if you please, she sent for her box. And not so much as a line to me! If I'd been at home, I'd not have let it go—treating me like that! But I'd just stepped out to the butcher."

"Will you describe her to me?"

"She was middle-aged, stout, black hair turning grey—most respectable. She'd been ten years in her last place. Eliza Dunn, her name was."

"And you had had—no disagreement with her on the Wednesday?"

"None whatsoever. That's what makes it all so queer."

"How many servants do you keep, madame?"

"Two. The house-parlourmaid, Annie, is a very nice girl. A bit forgetful and her head full of young men, but a good servant if you keep her up to her work."

"Did she and the cook get on well together?"

"They had their ups and downs, of course—but on the whole, very well."

"And the girl can throw no light on the mystery?"

"She says not—but you know what servants are—they all hang together."

"Well, well, we must look into this. Where did you say you resided, madame?"

"At Clapham; 88 Prince Albert Road."

"Bien, madame, I will wish you good morning, and you may count upon seeing me at your residence during the course of the day."

Mrs. Todd, for such was our new friend's name, then took her departure. Poirot looked at me somewhat ruefully.

"Well, well, Hastings, this is a novel affair that we have here. The Disappearance of the Clapham Cook! Never, never, must our friend Inspector Japp get to hear of this!"

He then proceeded to heat an iron and carefully removed the grease spot from his grey suit by means of a piece of blotting paper. His moustaches he regretfully postponed to another day, and we set out for Clapham.

Prince Albert Road proved to be a street of small prim houses, all exactly alike, with neat lace curtains veiling the windows, and well-polished brass knockers on the doors.

We rang the bell at No. 88, and the door was opened by a neat maid with a pretty face. Mrs. Todd came out in the hall to greet us.

"Don't go, Annie," she cried. "This gentleman's a detective and he'll want to ask you some questions."

Annie's face displayed a struggle between alarm and a pleasurable excitement.

"I thank you, madame," said Poirot bowing. "I would like to question your maid now—and to see her alone, if I may."

We were shown into a small drawing room, and when Mrs. Todd, with obvious reluctance, had left the room, Poirot commenced his cross-examination.

"Voyons, Mademoiselle Annie, all that you shall tell us will be of the greatest importance. You alone can shed any light on the case. Without your assistance I can do nothing."

The alarm vanished from the girl's face and the pleasurable excitement became more strongly marked.

"I'm sure, sir," she said, "I'll tell you anything I can."

"That is good." Poirot beamed approval on her. "Now, first of all what is your own idea? You are a girl of remarkable intelligence. That can be seen at once! What is your own explanation of Eliza's disappearance?"

Thus encouraged, Annie fairly flowed into excited speech.

"White slavers, sir, I've said so all along! Cook was always warning me against them. 'Don't you sniff no scent, or eat any sweets—no matter how gentlemanly the fellow!' Those were her words to me. And now they've got her! I'm sure of it. As likely as not, she's been shipped to Turkey or one of them Eastern places where I've heard they like them fat!"

Poirot preserved an admirable gravity.

"But in that case—and it is indeed an idea!—would she have sent for her trunk?"

"Well, I don't know, sir. She'd want her things—even in those foreign places."

"Who came for the trunk—a man?"

"It was Carter Paterson, sir."

"Did you pack it?"

"No, sir, it was already packed and corded."

"Ah! That's interesting. That shows that when she left the house on Wednesday, she had already determined not to return. You see that, do you not?"

"Yes, sir." Annie looked slightly taken aback. "I hadn't thought of that. But it might still have been white slavers, mightn't it, sir?" she added wistfully.

"Undoubtedly!" said Poirot gravely. He went on: "Did you both occupy the same bedroom?"

"No, sir, we had separate rooms."

"And had Eliza expressed any dissatisfaction with her present post to you at all? Were you both happy here?"

"She'd never mentioned leaving. The place is all right—" The girl hesitated.

"Speak freely," said Poirot kindly. "I shall not tell your mistress."

"Well, of course, sir, she's a caution, Missus is. But the food's good. Plenty of it, and no stinting. Something hot for supper, good outings, and as much frying-fat as you like. And anyway, if Eliza did want to make a change, she'd never have gone off this way, I'm sure. She'd have stayed her month. Why, Missus could have a month's wages out of her for doing this!"

"And the work, it is not too hard?"

"Well, she's particular—always poking round in corners and looking for dust. And then there's the lodger, or paying guest as he's always called. But that's only breakfast and dinner, same as Master. They're out all day in the City."

"You like your master?"

"He's all right—very quiet and a bit on the stingy side."

"You can't remember, I suppose, the last thing Eliza said before she went out?"

"Yes, I can. 'If there's any stewed peaches over from the dining room,' she says, 'we'll have them for supper, and a bit of bacon and some fried potatoes.' Mad over stewed peaches, she was. I shouldn't wonder if they didn't get her that way."

"Was Wednesday her regular day out?"

"Yes, she had Wednesdays and I had Thursdays."

Poirot asked a few more questions, then declared himself satisfied. Annie departed, and Mrs. Todd hurried in, her face alight with curiosity. She had, I felt certain, bitterly resented her exclusion from the room during our conversation with Annie. Poirot, however, was careful to soothe her feelings tactfully.

"It is difficult," he explained, "for a woman of exceptional intelligence such as yourself, madame, to bear patiently the roundabout methods we poor detectives are forced to use. To have patience with stupidity is difficult for the quick-witted."

Having thus charmed away any little resentment on Mrs. Todd's part, he brought the conversation round to her husband and elicited

 The Missing Will & Other Stories

the information that he worked with a firm in the City and would not be home until after six.

"Doubtless he is very disturbed and worried by this unaccountable business, eh? It is not so?"

"He's never worried," declared Mrs. Todd. " 'Well, well, get another, my dear.' That's all he said! He's so calm that it drives me to distraction sometimes. 'An ungrateful woman,' he said. 'We are well rid of her.' "

"What about the other inmates of the house, madame?"

"You mean Mr. Simpson, our paying guest? Well, as long as he gets his breakfast and his evening meal all right, he doesn't worry."

"What is his profession, madame?"

"He works in a bank." She mentioned its name, and I started slightly, remembering my perusal of the Daily Blare.

"A young man?"

"Twenty-eight, I believe. Nice quiet young fellow."

"I should like to have a few words with him, and also with your husband, if I may. I will return for that purpose this evening. I venture to suggest that you should repose yourself a little, madame, you look fatigued."

"I should just think I am! First the worry about Eliza, and then I was at the sales practically all yesterday, and you know what that is, M. Poirot, and what with one thing and another and a lot to do in the house, because of course Annie can't do it all—and very likely she'll give notice anyway, being unsettled in this way—well, what with it all, I'm tired out!"

Poirot murmured sympathetically, and we took our leave.

"It's a curious coincidence," I said, "but that absconding clerk, Davis, was from the same bank as Simpson. Can there be any connection, do you think?"

Poirot smiled.

"At the one end, a defaulting clerk, at the other a vanishing cook. It is hard to see any relation between the two, unless possibly Davis visited Simpson, fell in love with the cook, and persuaded her to accompany him on his flight!"

I laughed. But Poirot remained grave.

"He might have done worse," he said reprovingly. "Remember, Hastings, if you are going into exile, a good cook may be of more comfort than a pretty face!" He paused for a moment and then went on. "It is a curious case, full of contradictory features. I am interested—yes, I am distinctly interested."

II

That evening we returned to 88 Prince Albert Road and interviewed both Todd and Simpson. The former was a melancholy lantern-jawed man of forty-odd.

"Oh! Yes, yes," he said vaguely. "Eliza. Yes. A good cook, I believe. And economical. I make a strong point of economy."

"Can you imagine any reason for her leaving you so suddenly?"

"Oh, well," said Mr. Todd vaguely. "Servants, you know. My wife worries too much. Worn out from always worrying. The whole problem's quite simple really. 'Get another, my dear,' I say. 'Get another.' That's all there is to it. No good crying over spilt milk."

Mr. Simpson was equally unhelpful. He was a quiet inconspicuous young man with spectacles.

"I must have seen her, I suppose," he said. "Elderly woman, wasn't she? Of course, it's the other one I see always, Annie. Nice girl. Very obliging."

"Were those two on good terms with each other?"

Mr. Simpson said he couldn't say, he was sure. He supposed so.

"Well, we get nothing of interest there, mon ami," said Poirot as we left the house. Our departure had been delayed by a burst of vociferous repetition from Mrs. Todd, who repeated everything she had said that morning at rather greater length.

"Are you disappointed?" I asked. "Did you expect to hear something?"

Poirot shook his head.

"There was a possibility, of course," he said. "But I hardly thought it likely."

The next development was a letter which Poirot received on the following morning. He read it, turned purple with indignation, and handed it to me.

Mrs. Todd regrets that after all she will not avail herself of Mr. Poirot's services. After talking the matter over with her husband she sees that it is foolish to call in a detective about a purely domestic affair. Mrs. Todd encloses a guinea for consultation fee.

III

"Aha!" cried Poirot angrily. "And they think to get rid of Hercule Poirot like that! As a favour—a great favour—I consent to investigate their miserable little twopenny-halfpenny affair—and they dismiss me comme ça! Here, I mistake not, is the hand of Mr. Todd. But I say no!—thirty-six times no! I will spend my own guineas, thirty-six hundred of them if need be, but I will get to the bottom of this matter!"

"Yes," I said. "But how?"

Poirot calmed down a little.

"D'abord," he said, "we will advertise in the papers. Let me see—yes—something like this: 'If Eliza Dunn will communicate with this address, she will hear of something to her advantage.' Put it in all the papers you can think of, Hastings. Then I will make some little inquiries of my own. Go, go—all must be done as quickly as possible!"

I did not see him again until the evening, when he condescended to tell me what he had been doing.

"I have made inquiries at the firm of Mr. Todd. He was not absent on Wednesday, and he bears a good character—so much for him. Then Simpson, on Thursday he was ill and did not come to the bank, but he was there on Wednesday. He was moderately friendly with Davis. Nothing out of the common. There does not seem to be anything there. No. We must place our reliance on the advertisement."

The advertisement duly appeared in all the principal daily papers. By Poirot's orders it was to be continued every day for a week. His eagerness over this uninteresting matter of a defaulting cook was extraordinary, but I realized that he considered it a point of honour to persevere until he finally succeeded. Several extremely interesting cases were brought to him about this time, but he declined them all. Every morning he would rush at his letters, scrutinize them earnestly and then lay them down with a sigh.

But our patience was rewarded at last. On the Wednesday following Mrs. Todd's visit, our landlady informed us that a person of the name of Eliza Dunn had called.

"Enfin!" cried Poirot. "But make her mount then! At once. Immediately."

Thus admonished, our landlady hurried out and returned a moment or two later, ushering in Miss Dunn. Our quarry was much as described: tall, stout, and eminently respectable.

"I came in answer to the advertisement," she explained. "I thought there must be some muddle or other, and that perhaps you didn't know I'd already got my legacy."

Poirot was studying her attentively. He drew forward a chair with a flourish.

"The truth of the matter is," he explained, "that your late mistress, Mrs. Todd, was much concerned about you. She feared some accident might have befallen you."

Eliza Dunn seemed very much surprised.

"Didn't she get my letter then?"

"She got no word of any kind." He paused, and then said persuasively: "Recount to me the whole story, will you not?"

Eliza Dunn needed no encouragement. She plunged at once into a lengthy narrative.

"I was just coming home on Wednesday night and had nearly got to the house, when a gentleman stopped me. A tall gentleman he was, with a beard and a big hat. 'Miss Eliza Dunn?' he said. 'Yes,' I said. 'I've been inquiring for you at No. 88,' he said. 'They told me I might meet you coming along here. Miss Dunn, I have come from Australia specially to find you. Do you happen to know the maiden name of your maternal grandmother?' 'Jane Emmott,' I said. 'Exactly,' he said. 'Now, Miss Dunn, although you may never have heard of the fact, your grandmother had a great friend, Eliza Leech. This friend went to Australia where she married a very wealthy settler. Her two children died in infancy, and she inherited all her husband's property. She died a few months ago, and by her will you inherit a house in this country and a considerable sum of money.'

"You could have knocked me down with a feather," continued Miss Dunn. "For a minute, I was suspicious, and he must have seen it, for he smiled. 'Quite right to be on your guard, Miss Dunn,' he said. 'Here are my credentials.' He handed me a letter from some lawyers in Melbourne, Hurst and Crotchet, and a card. He was Mr. Crotchet. 'There are one or two conditions,' he said. 'Our client was a little eccentric, you know. The bequest is conditional on your taking possession of the house (it is in Cumberland) before twelve o'clock tomorrow. The other condition is of no importance—it is merely a stipulation that you should not be in domestic service.' My face fell. 'Oh, Mr. Crotchet,' I said. 'I'm a cook. Didn't they tell you at the house?' 'Dear, dear,' he said. 'I had no idea of such a thing. I thought you might possibly be a companion or governess there. This is very unfortunate—very unfortunate indeed.'

" 'Shall I have to lose all the money?' I said, anxious like. He thought for a minute or two. 'There are always ways of getting round the law, Miss Dunn,' he said at last. 'We as lawyers know that. The way out here is for you to have left your employment this afternoon.' 'But my month?' I said. 'My dear Miss Dunn,' he said with a smile. 'You can leave an employer any minute by forfeiting a month's wages. Your mistress will understand in view of the circumstances. The difficulty is time! It is imperative that you should catch the 11.05 from King's Cross to the north. I can advance you ten pounds or so for the fare, and you can write a note at the station to your employer. I will take it to her myself and explain the whole circumstances.' I agreed, of course, and an hour later I was in the train, so flustered that I didn't know whether I was on my head or heels. Indeed by the time I got to Carlisle, I was half inclined to think the whole thing was one of those confidence tricks you read about. But I went to the address he had given me—solicitors they were, and it was all right. A nice little house, and an income of three hundred a year. These lawyers knew very little, they'd just got a letter from a gentleman in London instructing them to hand over the house to me and £150 for the first six months. Mr. Crotchet sent up my things to me, but there was no word from Missus. I supposed she was angry and grudged me my bit of luck. She kept back my box too, and sent my clothes in paper parcels. But there, of course if she never had my letter, she might think it a bit cool of me."

Poirot had listened attentively to this long history. Now he nodded his head as though completely satisfied.

"Thank you, mademoiselle. There had been, as you say, a little muddle. Permit me to recompense you for your trouble." He handed her an envelope. "You return to Cumberland immediately? A little word in your ear. Do not forget how to cook. It is always useful to have something to fall back upon in case things go wrong."

"Credulous," he murmured, as our visitor departed, "but perhaps not more than most of her class." His face grew grave. "Come, Hastings, there is no time to be lost. Get a taxi while I write a note to Japp."

                                    The Missing Will & Other Stories

Poirot was waiting on the doorstep when I returned with the taxi.

"Where are we going?" I asked anxiously.

"First, to despatch this note by special messenger."

This was done, and reentering the taxi Poirot gave the address to the driver.

"Eighty-eight Prince Albert Road, Clapham."

"So we are going there?"

"Mais oui. Though frankly I fear we shall be too late. Our bird will have flown, Hastings."

"Who is our bird?"

Poirot smiled.

"The inconspicuous Mr. Simpson."

"What?" I exclaimed.

"Oh, come now, Hastings, do not tell me that all is not clear to you now!"

"The cook was got out of the way, I realize that," I said, slightly piqued. "But why? Why should Simpson wish to get her out of the house? Did she know something about him?"

"Nothing whatever."

"Well, then—"

"But he wanted something that she had."

"Money? The Australian legacy?"

"No, my friend—something quite different." He paused a moment and then said gravely: "A battered tin trunk. . . ."

I looked sideways at him. His statement seemed so fantastic that I suspected him of pulling my leg, but he was perfectly grave and serious.

"Surely he could buy a trunk if he wanted one," I cried.

"He did not want a new trunk. He wanted a trunk of pedigree. A trunk of assured respectability."

"Look here, Poirot," I cried, "this really is a bit thick. You're pulling my leg."

He looked at me.

"You lack the brains and the imagination of Mr. Simpson, Hastings. See here: On Wednesday evening, Simpson decoys away the cook. A printed card and a printed sheet of notepaper are simple matters to obtain, and he is willing to pay £150 and a year's house rent to assure the success of his plan. Miss Dunn does not recognize him—the beard and the hat and the slight colonial accent completely deceive her. That is the end of Wednesday—except for the trifling fact that Simpson has helped himself to fifty thousand pounds' worth of negotiable securities."

"Simpson—but it was Davis—"

"If you will kindly permit me to continue, Hastings! Simpson knows that the theft will be discovered on Thursday afternoon. He does not go to the bank on Thursday, but he lies in wait for Davis when he comes out to lunch. Perhaps he admits the theft and tells Davis he will return the securities to him—anyhow he succeeds in getting Davis to come to Clapham with him. It is the maid's day out, and Mrs. Todd was at the sales, so there is no one in the house. When the theft is discovered and Davis is missing, the implication will be overwhelming. Davis is the thief! Mr. Simpson will be perfectly safe, and can return to work on the morrow like the honest clerk they think him."

"And Davis?"

Poirot made an expressive gesture, and slowly shook his head.

"It seems too cold-blooded to be believed, and yet what other explanation can there be, mon ami. The one difficulty for a murderer is the disposal of the body—and Simpson had planned that out beforehand. I was struck at once by the fact that although Eliza Dunn obviously meant to return that night when she went out (witness her remark about the stewed peaches) yet her trunk was all ready packed when they came for it. It was Simpson who sent word to Carter Paterson to call on Friday and it was Simpson who corded up the box on Thursday afternoon. What suspicion could possibly arise? A maid leaves and sends for her box, it is labelled and addressed ready in her name, probably to a railway station within easy reach of London. On Saturday afternoon, Simpson, in his Australian disguise, claims it, he affixes a new label and address and redespatches it somewhere else, again 'to be left till called for.' When the authorities get suspicious, for excellent reasons, and open it, all that can be elicited will be that a bearded colonial despatched it from some junction near London. There will be nothing to connect it with 88 Prince Albert Road. Ah! Here we are."

Poirot's prognostications had been correct. Simpson had left days previously. But he was not to escape the consequences of his crime. By the aid of wireless, he was discovered on the Olympia, en route to America.

A tin trunk, addressed to Mr. Henry Wintergreen, attracted the attention of railway officials at Glasgow. It was opened and found to contain the body of the unfortunate Davis.

Mrs. Todd's cheque for a guinea was never cashed. Instead Poirot had it framed and hung on the wall of our sitting room.

"It is to me a little reminder, Hastings. Never to despise the trivial— the undignified. A disappearing domestic at one end—a cold-blooded murder at the other. To me, one of the most interesting of my cases."

The Lost Mine

I laid down my bank book with a sigh.

"It is a curious thing," I observed, "but my overdraft never seems to grow any less."

"And it perturbs you not? Me, if I had an overdraft, never should I close my eyes all night," declared Poirot.

"You deal in comfortable balances, I suppose!" I retorted.

"Four hundred and forty-four pounds, four and fourpence," said Poirot with some complacency. "A neat figure, is it not?"

"It must be tact on the part of your bank manager. He is evidently acquainted with your passion for symmetrical details. What about investing, say, three hundred of it in the Porcupine oil fields? Their prospectus, which is advertised in the papers today, says that they will pay one hundred per cent dividends next year."

"Not for me," said Poirot, shaking his head. "I like not the sensational. For me the safe, the prudent investment—les rentes, the consols, the—how do you call it?—the conversion."

"Have you never made a speculative investment?"

"No, mon ami," replied Poirot severely. "I have not. And the only shares I own which have not what you call the gilded edge are fourteen thousand shares in the Burma Mines Ltd."

Poirot paused with an air of waiting to be encouraged to go on.

"Yes?" I prompted.

"And for them I paid no cash—no, they were the reward of the exercise of my little grey cells. You would like to hear the story? Yes?"

"Of course I would."

"These mines are situated in the interior of Burma about two hundred miles inland from Rangoon. They were discovered by the Chinese in the fifteenth century and worked down to the time of the Mohammedan Rebellion, being finally abandoned in the year 1868. The Chinese extracted the rich lead-silver ore from the upper part of the ore body, smelting it for the silver alone, and leaving large quantities of rich lead-bearing slag. This, of course, was soon discovered when prospecting work was carried out in Burma, but owing to the fact that the old workings had become full of loose filling and water, all attempts to find the source of the ore proved fruitless. Many parties were sent out by syndicates, and they dug over a large area, but this rich prize still eluded them. But a representative of one of the syndicates got on the track of a Chinese family who were supposed to have still kept a record of the situation of the mine. The present head of the family was one Wu Ling."

"What a fascinating page of commercial romance!" I exclaimed.

"Is it not? Ah, mon ami, one can have romance without golden-haired girls of matchless beauty—no, I am wrong; it is auburn hair that so excites you always. You remember—"

"Go on with the story," I said hastily.

"Eh bien, my friend, this Wu Ling was approached. He was an estimable merchant, much respected in the province where he lived. He admitted at once that he owned the documents in question, and was perfectly prepared to negotiate for this sale, but he objected to dealing with anyone other than principals. Finally it was arranged that he should journey to England and meet the directors of an important company.

"Wu Ling made the journey to England in the SS Assunta, and the Assunta docked at Southampton on a cold, foggy morning in November. One of the directors, Mr. Pearson, went down to Southampton to meet the boat, but owing to the fog, the train down was very much delayed, and by the time he arrived, Wu Ling had disembarked and left by special train for London. Mr. Pearson returned to town somewhat annoyed, as he had no idea where the Chinaman proposed to stay. Later in the day, however, the offices of the company were rung up on the telephone. Wu Ling was staying at the Russell Square Hotel. He was feeling somewhat unwell after the voyage, but declared himself perfectly able to attend the board meeting on the following day.

"The meeting of the board took place at eleven o'clock. When half past eleven came, and Wu Ling had not put in an appearance, the secretary rang up the Russell Hotel. In answer to his inquiries, he was told that the Chinaman had gone out with a friend about half past ten. It seemed clear that he had started out with the intention of coming to the meeting, but the morning wore away, and he did not appear. It was, of course, possible that he had lost his way, being unacquainted with London, but at a late hour that night he had not returned to the hotel. Thoroughly alarmed now, Mr. Pearson put matters in the hands of the police. On the following day, there was still no trace of the missing man, but towards evening of the day after that again, a body was found in the Thames which proved to be that of the ill-fated Chinaman. Neither on the body, nor in the luggage at the hotel, was there any trace of the papers relating to the mine.

"At this juncture, mon ami, I was brought into the affair. Mr. Pearson called upon me. While profoundly shocked by the death of Wu Ling, his chief anxiety was to recover the papers which were the object of the Chinaman's visit to England. The main anxiety of the police, of course, would be to track down the murderer—the recovery of the papers would be a secondary consideration. What he wanted me to do was to cooperate with the police while acting in the interests of the company.

                                    The Missing Will & Other Stories

"I consented readily enough. It was clear that there were two fields of search open to me. On the one hand, I might look among the employees of the company who knew of the Chinaman's coming; on the other, among the passengers on the boat who might have been acquainted with his mission. I started with the second, as being a narrower field of search. In this I coincided with Inspector Miller, who was in charge of the case—a man altogether different from our friend Japp, conceited, ill-mannered and quite insufferable. Together we interviewed the officers of the ship. They had little to tell us. Wu Ling had kept much to himself on the voyage. He had been intimate with but two of the other passengers—one a broken-down European named Dyer who appeared to bear a somewhat unsavoury reputation, the other a young bank clerk named Charles Lester, who was returning from Hong Kong. We were lucky enough to obtain snapshots of both these men. At the moment there seemed little doubt that if either of the two was implicated, Dyer was the man. He was known to be mixed up with a gang of Chinese crooks, and was altogether a most likely suspect.

"Our next step was to visit the Russell Square Hotel. Shown a snapshot of Wu Ling, they recognized him at once. We then showed them the snapshot of Dyer, but to our disappointment, the hall porter declared positively that that was not the man who had come to the hotel on the fatal morning. Almost as an afterthought, I produced the photograph of Lester, and to my surprise the man at once recognized it.

" 'Yes, sir,' he asserted, 'that's the gentleman who came in at half past ten and asked for Mr. Wu Ling, and afterwards went out with him.'

"The affair was progressing. Our next move was to interview Mr. Charles Lester. He met us with the utmost frankness, was desolated to hear of the Chinaman's untimely death, and put himself at our disposal in every way. His story was as follows: By arrangement with Wu Ling, he called for him at the hotel at ten thirty. Wu Ling, however, did not appear. Instead, his servant came, explained that his master had had to go out, and offered to conduct the young man to where his master now was. Suspecting nothing, Lester agreed, and the Chinaman procured a taxi. They drove for some time in the direction of the docks. Suddenly becoming mistrustful, Lester stopped the taxi and got out, disregarding the servant's protests. That, he assured us, was all he knew.

"Apparently satisfied, we thanked him and took our leave. His story was soon proved to be a somewhat inaccurate one. To begin with, Wu Ling had had no servant with him, either on the boat or at the hotel. In the second place, the taxi driver who had driven the two men on that morning came forward. Far from Lester's having left the taxi en route, he and the Chinese gentleman had driven to a certain unsavoury dwelling place in Limehouse, right in the heart of Chinatown. The place in question was more or less well known as an opium den of the lowest description. The two gentlemen had gone in—about an hour later the English gentleman, whom he identified from the photograph, came out alone. He looked very pale and ill, and directed the taxi man to take him to the nearest underground station.

"Inquiries were made about Charles Lester's standing, and it was found that, though bearing an excellent character, he was heavily in debt, and had a secret passion for gambling. Dyer, of course, was not lost sight of. It seemed just faintly possible that he might have impersonated the other man, but that idea was proved utterly groundless. His alibi for the whole of the day in question was absolutely unimpeachable. Of course, the proprietor of the opium den denied everything with Oriental stolidity. He had never seen Charles Lester. No two gentlemen had been to the place that morning. In any case, the police were wrong: no opium was ever smoked there.

"His denials, however well meant, did little to help Charles Lester. He was arrested for the murder of Wu Ling. A search of his effects was made, but no papers relating to the mine were discovered. The proprietor of the opium den was also taken into custody, but a cursory raid of his premises yielded nothing. Not even a stick of opium rewarded the zeal of the police.

                    The Missing Will & Other Stories

"In the meantime my friend Mr. Pearson was in a great state of agitation. He strode up and down my room, uttering great lamentations.

"'But you must have some ideas, M. Poirot!' he kept urging. 'Surely you must have some ideas!'

"'Certainly I have ideas,' I replied cautiously. 'That is the trouble—one has too many; therefore they all lead in different directions.'

"'For instance?' he suggested.

"'For instance—the taxi driver. We have only his word for it that he drove the two men to that house. That is one idea. Then—was it really that house they went to? Supposing that they left the taxi there, passed through the house and out by another entrance and went elsewhere?'

"Mr. Pearson seemed struck by that.

" 'But you do nothing but sit and think? Can't we do something?'

"He was of an impatient temperament, you comprehend.

" 'Monsieur,' I said with dignity, 'It is not for Hercule Poirot to run up and down the evil-smelling streets of Limehouse like a little dog of no breeding. Be calm. My agents are at work.'

"On the following day I had news for him. The two men had indeed passed through the house in question, but their real objective was a small eating house close to the river. They were seen to pass in there, and Lester came out alone.

"And then, figure to yourself, Hastings, an idea of the most unreasonable seized this Mr. Pearson! Nothing would suit him but that we should go ourselves to this eating house and make investigations. I argued and prayed, but he would not listen. He talked of disguising himself—he even suggested that I—I should—I hesitate to say it—should shave off my moustache! Yes, rien que ça! I pointed out to him that that was an idea ridiculous and absurd. One destroys not a thing of beauty wantonly. Besides, shall not a Belgian gentleman with a moustache desire to see life and smoke opium just as readily as one without a moustache?

"Eh bien, he gave in on that, but he still insisted on his project. He turned up that evening—Mon dieu, what a figure! He wore what he called the 'pea jacket,' his chin, it was dirty and unshaved; he had a scarf of the vilest that offended the nose. And figure to yourself, he was enjoying himself! Truly, the English are mad! He made some changes in my own appearance. I permitted it. Can one argue with a maniac? We started out—after all, could I let him go alone, a child dressed up to act the charades?"

"Of course you couldn't," I replied.

"To continue—we arrived. Mr. Pearson talked English of the strangest. He represented himself to be a man of the sea. He talked of 'lubbers' and 'focselles' and I know not what. It was a low little room with many Chinese in it. We ate of peculiar dishes. Ah, Dieu, mon estomac!" Poirot clasped that portion of his anatomy before continuing. "Then there came to us the proprietor, a Chinaman with a face of evil smiles.

" 'You gentlemen no likee food here,' he said. 'You come for what you likee better. Piecee pipe, eh?'

"Mr. Pearson, he gave me the great kick under the table. (He had on the boots of the sea too!) And he said: 'I don't mind if I do, John. Lead ahead.'

"The Chinaman smiled, and he took us through a door and to a cellar and through a trapdoor, and down some steps and up again into a room all full of divans and cushions of the most comfortable. We lay down and a Chinese boy took off our boots. It was the best moment of the evening. Then they brought us the opium pipes and cooked the opium pills, and we pretended to smoke and then to sleep and dream. But when we were alone, Mr. Pearson called softly to me, and immediately he began crawling along the floor. We went into another room where other people were asleep, and so on, until we heard two men talking. We stayed behind a curtain and listened. They were speaking of Wu Ling.

The Missing Will & Other Stories

" 'What about the papers?' said one.

" 'Mr. Lester, he takee those,' answered the other, who was a Chinaman. 'He say, puttee them allee in safee place—where pleeceman no lookee.'

" 'Ah, but he's nabbed,' said the first one.

" 'He gettee free. Pleeceman not sure he done it.'

"There was more of the same kind of thing, then apparently the two men were coming our way, and we scuttled back to our beds.

" 'We'd better get out of here,' said Pearson, after a few minutes had elapsed. 'This place isn't healthy.'

" 'You are right, monsieur,' I agreed. 'We have played the farce long enough.'

"We succeeded in getting away, all right, paying handsomely for our smoke. Once clear of Limehouse, Pearson drew a long breath.

" 'I'm glad to get out of that,' he said. 'But it's something to be sure.'

" 'It is indeed,' I agreed. 'And I fancy that we shall not have much difficulty in finding what we want—after this evening's masquerade.'

"And there was no difficulty whatsoever," finished Poirot suddenly.

This abrupt ending seemed so extraordinary that I stared at him.

"But—but where were they?" I asked.

"In his pocket—tout simplement."

"But in whose pocket?"

"Mr. Pearson's, parbleu!" Then, observing my look of bewilderment, he continued gently: "You do not yet see it? Mr. Pearson, like Charles Lester, was in debt. Mr. Pearson, like Charles Lester, was fond of gambling. And he conceived the idea of stealing the papers from the Chinaman. He met him all right at Southampton, came up to London with him, and took him straight to Limehouse. It was foggy that day; the Chinaman would not notice where he was going. I fancy

Mr. Pearson smoked the opium fairly often down there and had some peculiar friends in consequence. I do not think he meant murder. His idea was that one of the Chinamen should impersonate Wu Ling and receive the money for the sale of the document. So far, so good! But, to the Oriental mind, it was infinitely simpler to kill Wu Ling and throw his body into the river, and Pearson's Chinese accomplices followed their own methods without consulting him. Imagine, then, what you would call the 'funk bleu' of M. Pearson. Someone may have seen him in the train with Wu Ling—murder is a very different thing from simple abduction.

"His salvation lies with the Chinaman who is personating Wu Ling at the Russell Square Hotel. If only the body is not discovered too soon! Probably Wu Ling had told him of the arrangement between him and Charles Lester whereby the latter was to call for him at the hotel. Pearson sees there an excellent way of diverting suspicion from himself. Charles Lester shall be the last person to be seen in company with Wu Ling. The impersonator has orders to represent himself to Lester as the servant of Wu Ling, and to bring him as speedily as possible to Limehouse. There, very likely, he was offered a drink. The drink would be suitably drugged, and when Lester emerged an hour later, he would have a very hazy impression of what had happened. So much was this the case, that as soon as Lester learned of Wu Ling's death, he loses his nerve, and denies that he ever reached Limehouse.

"By that, of course, he plays right into Pearson's hands. But is Pearson content? No—my manner disquiets him, and he determines to complete the case against Lester. So he arranges an elaborate masquerade. Me, I am to be gulled completely. Did I not say just now that he was as a child acting the charades? Eh bien, I play my part. He goes home rejoicing. But in the morning, Inspector Miller arrives on his doorstep. The papers are found on him; the game is up. Bitterly he regrets permitting himself to play the farce with Hercule Poirot! There was only one real difficulty in the affair."

"What was that?" I demanded curiously.

"Convincing Inspector Miller! What an animal, that! Both obstinate and imbecile. And in the end he took all the credit!"

"Too bad," I cried.

"Ah, well, I had my compensations. The other directors of the Burma Mines Ltd. awarded me fourteen thousand shares as a small recompense for my services. Not so bad, eh? But when investing money, keep, I beg of you, Hastings, strictly to the conservative. The things you read in the paper, they may not be true. The directors of the Porcupine—they may be so many Mr. Pearsons!"

The Theft of the Royal Ruby

"I regret exceedingly—" said M. Hercule Poirot.

He was interrupted. Not rudely interrupted. The interruption was suave, dexterous, persuasive rather than contradictory.

"Please don't refuse offhand, M. Poirot. There are grave issues of State. Your cooperation will be appreciated in the highest quarters."

"You are too kind," Hercule Poirot waved a hand, "but I really cannot undertake to do as you ask. At this season of the year—"

Again Mr. Jesmond interrupted. "Christmastime," he said, persuasively. "An old-fashioned Christmas in the English countryside."

Hercule Poirot shivered. The thought of the English countryside at this season of the year did not attract him.

"A good old-fashioned Christmas!" Mr. Jesmond stressed it.

"Me—I am not an Englishman," said Hercule Poirot. "In my country, Christmas, it is for the children. The New Year, that is what we celebrate."

"Ah," said Mr. Jesmond, "but Christmas in England is a great institution and I assure you at Kings Lacey you would see it at its best. It's a wonderful old house, you know. Why, one wing of it dates from the fourteenth century."

Again Poirot shivered. The thought of a fourteenth-century English manor house filled him with apprehension. He had suffered too often in the historic country houses of England. He looked round appreciatively at his comfortable modern flat with its radiators and the latest patent devices for excluding any kind of draught.

"In the winter," he said firmly, "I do not leave London."

"I don't think you quite appreciate, M. Poirot, what a very serious matter this is." Mr. Jesmond glanced at his companion and then back at Poirot.

Poirot's second visitor had up to now said nothing but a polite and formal "How do you do." He sat now, gazing down at his well-polished shoes, with an air of the utmost dejection on his coffee-coloured face. He was a young man, not more than twenty-three, and he was clearly in a state of complete misery.

"Yes, yes," said Hercule Poirot. "Of course the matter is serious. I do appreciate that. His Highness has my heartfelt sympathy."

"The position is one of the utmost delicacy," said Mr. Jesmond.

Poirot transferred his gaze from the young man to his older companion. If one wanted to sum up Mr. Jesmond in a word, the word would have been discretion. Everything about Mr. Jesmond was discreet. His well-cut but inconspicuous clothes, his pleasant, well-bred voice which rarely soared out of an agreeable monotone, his light-brown hair just thinning a little at the temples, his pale serious face. It seemed to Hercule Poirot that he had known not one Mr. Jesmond but a dozen Mr. Jesmonds in his time, all using sooner or later the same phrase—"a position of the utmost delicacy."

"The police," said Hercule Poirot, "can be very discreet, you know."

Mr. Jesmond shook his head firmly.

"Not the police," he said. "To recover the—er—what we want to recover will almost inevitably invoke taking proceedings in the law courts and we know so little. We suspect, but we do not know."

"You have my sympathy," said Hercule Poirot again.

If he imagined that his sympathy was going to mean anything to his two visitors, he was wrong. They did not want sympathy, they wanted practical help. Mr. Jesmond began once more to talk about the delights of an English Christmas.

"It's dying out, you know," he said, "the real old-fashioned type of Christmas. People spend it at hotels nowadays. But an English Christmas with all the family gathered round, the children and their stockings, the Christmas tree, the turkey and plum pudding, the crackers. The snowman outside the window—"

In the interests of exactitude, Hercule Poirot intervened.

"To make a snowman one has to have the snow," he remarked severely. "And one cannot have snow to order, even for an English Christmas."

"I was talking to a friend of mine in the meteorological office only today," said Mr. Jesmond, "and he tells me that it is highly probable there will be snow this Christmas."

It was the wrong thing to have said. Hercule Poirot shuddered more forcefully than ever.

"Snow in the country!" he said. "That would be still more abominable. A large, cold, stone manor house."

"Not at all," said Mr. Jesmond. "Things have changed very much in the last ten years or so. Oil-fired central heating."

"They have oil-fired central heating at Kings Lacey?" asked Poirot. For the first time he seemed to waver.

Mr. Jesmond seized his opportunity. "Yes, indeed," he said, "and a splendid hot water system. Radiators in every bedroom. I assure you, my dear M. Poirot, Kings Lacey is comfort itself in the wintertime. You might even find the house too warm."

"That is most unlikely," said Hercule Poirot.

With practised dexterity Mr. Jesmond shifted his ground a little.

"You can appreciate the terrible dilemma we are in," he said, in a confidential manner.

Hercule Poirot nodded. The problem was, indeed, not a happy one. A young potentate-to-be, the only son of the ruler of a rich

The Missing Will & Other Stories

and important native State had arrived in London a few weeks ago. His country had been passing through a period of restlessness and discontent. Though loyal to the father whose way of life had remained persistently Eastern, popular opinion was somewhat dubious of the younger generation. His follies had been Western ones and as such looked upon with disapproval.

Recently, however, his betrothal had been announced. He was to marry a cousin of the same blood, a young woman who, though educated at Cambridge, was careful to display no Western influence in her own country. The wedding day was announced and the young prince had made a journey to England, bringing with him some of the famous jewels of his house to be reset in appropriate modern settings by Cartier. These had included a very famous ruby which had been removed from its cumbersome old-fashioned necklace and had been given a new look by the famous jewellers. So far so good, but after this came the snag. It was not to be supposed that a young man possessed of much wealth and convivial tastes, should not commit a few follies of the pleasanter type. As to that there would have been no censure. Young princes were supposed to amuse themselves in this fashion. For the prince to take the girlfriend of the moment for a walk down Bond Street and bestow upon her an emerald bracelet or a diamond clip as a reward for the pleasure she had afforded him would have been regarded as quite natural and suitable, corresponding in fact to the Cadillac cars which his father invariably presented to his favourite dancing girl of the moment.

But the prince had been far more indiscreet than that. Flattered by the lady's interest, he had displayed to her the famous ruby in its new setting, and had finally been so unwise as to accede to her request to be allowed to wear it—just for one evening!

The sequel was short and sad. The lady had retired from their supper table to powder her nose. Time passed. She did not return. She had left the establishment by another door and since then had disappeared into space. The important and distressing thing was that the ruby in its new setting had disappeared with her.

These were the facts that could not possibly be made public without the most dire consequences. The ruby was something more than a ruby, it was a historical possession of great significance, and the circumstances of its disappearance were such that any undue publicity about them might result in the most serious political consequences.

Mr. Jesmond was not the man to put these facts into simple language. He wrapped them up, as it were, in a great deal of verbiage. Who exactly Mr. Jesmond was, Hercule Poirot did not know. He had met other Mr. Jesmonds in the course of his career. Whether he was connected with the Home Office, the Foreign Secretary or some other discreet branch of public service was not specified. He was acting in the interests of the Commonwealth. The ruby must be recovered.

M. Poirot, so Mr. Jesmond delicately insisted, was the man to recover it.

"Perhaps—yes," Hercule Poirot admitted, "but you can tell me so little. Suggestion—suspicion—all that is not very much to go upon."

"Come now, Monsieur Poirot, surely it is not beyond your powers. Ah, come now."

"I do not always succeed."

But this was mock modesty. It was clear enough from Poirot's tone that for him to undertake a mission was almost synonymous with succeeding in it.

"His Highness is very young," Mr. Jesmond said. "It will be sad if his whole life is to be blighted for a mere youthful indiscretion."

Poirot looked kindly at the downcast young man. "It is the time for follies, when one is young," he said encouragingly, "and for the ordinary young man it does not matter so much. The good papa, he pays up: the family lawyer, he helps to disentangle the inconvenience; the young man, he learns by experience and all ends for the best. In a position such as yours, it is hard indeed. Your approaching marriage—"

"That is it. That is it exactly." For the first time words poured from the young man. "You see she is very, very serious. She takes life very seriously. She has acquired at Cambridge many very serious ideas. There is to be education in my country. There are to be schools. There are to be many things. All in the name of progress, you understand, of democracy. It will not be, she says, like it was in my father's time. Naturally she knows that I will have diversions in London, but not the scandal. No! It is the scandal that matters. You see it is very, very famous, this ruby. There is a long trail behind it, a history. Much bloodshed—many deaths!"

"Deaths," said Hercule Poirot thoughtfully. He looked at Mr. Jesmond. "One hopes," he said, "it will not come to that?"

Mr. Jesmond made a peculiar noise rather like a hen who has decided to lay an egg and then thought better of it.

"No, no indeed," he said, sounding rather prim. "There is no question, I am sure, of anything of that kind."

"You cannot be sure," said Hercule Poirot. "Whoever has the ruby now, there may be others who want to gain possession of it, and who will not stick at a trifle, my friend."

"I really don't think," said Mr. Jesmond, sounding more prim than ever, "that we need enter into speculation of that kind. Quite unprofitable."

"Me," said Hercule Poirot, suddenly becoming very foreign, "me, I explore all the avenues, like the politicians."

Mr. Jesmond looked at him doubtfully. Pulling himself together, he said, "Well, I can take it that is settled, M. Poirot? You will go to Kings Lacey?"

"And how do I explain myself there?" asked Hercule Poirot.

Mr. Jesmond smiled with confidence.

"That, I think, can be arranged very easily," he said. "I can assure you that it will all seem quite natural. You will find the Laceys most charming. Delightful people."

"And you do not deceive me about the oil-fired central heating?"

"No, no, indeed." Mr. Jesmond sounded quite pained. "I assure you you will find every comfort."

"Tout confort moderne," murmured Poirot to himself, reminiscently. "Eh bien," he said, "I accept."

The temperature in the long drawing room at Kings Lacey was a comfortable sixty-eight as Hercule Poirot sat talking to Mrs. Lacey by one of the big mullioned windows. Mrs. Lacey was engaged in needlework. She was not doing petit point or embroidered flowers upon silk. Instead, she appeared to be engaged in the prosaic task of hemming dishcloths. As she sewed she talked in a soft reflective voice that Poirot found very charming.

"I hope you will enjoy our Christmas party here, M. Poirot. It's only the family, you know. My granddaughter and a grandson and a friend of his and Bridget who's my great niece, and Diana who's a cousin and David Welwyn who is a very old friend. Just a family party. But Edwina Morecombe said that that's what you really wanted to see. An old-fashioned Christmas. Nothing could be more old-fashioned than we are! My husband, you know, absolutely lives in the past. He likes everything to be just as it was when he was a boy of twelve years old, and used to come here for his holidays." She smiled to herself. "All the same old things, the Christmas tree and the stockings hung up and the oyster soup and the turkey—two turkeys, one boiled and one roast—and the plum pudding with the ring and the bachelor's button and all the rest of it in it. We can't have sixpences nowadays because they're not pure silver any more. But all the old desserts, the Elvas plums and Carlsbad plums and almonds and raisins, and crystallized fruit and ginger. Dear me, I sound like a catalogue from Fortnum and Mason!"

"You arouse my gastronomic juices, Madame."

"I expect we'll all have frightful indigestion by tomorrow evening," said Mrs. Lacey. "One isn't used to eating so much nowadays, is one?"

She was interrupted by some loud shouts and whoops of laughter outside the window. She glanced out.

"I don't know what they're doing out there. Playing some game or other, I suppose. I've always been so afraid, you know, that these young people would be bored by our Christmas here. But not at all, it's just the opposite. Now my own son and daughter and their friends, they used to be rather sophisticated about Christmas. Say it was all nonsense and too much fuss and it would be far better to go out to a hotel somewhere and dance. But the younger generation seem to find all this terribly attractive. Besides," added Mrs. Lacey practically, "schoolboys and schoolgirls are always hungry, aren't they? I think they must starve them at these schools. After all, one does know children of that age each eat about as much as three strong men."

Poirot laughed and said, "It is most kind of you and your husband, Madame, to include me in this way in your family party."

"Oh, we're both delighted, I'm sure," said Mrs. Lacey. "And if you find Horace a little gruff," she continued, "pay no attention. It's just his manner, you know."

What her husband, Colonel Lacey, had actually said was: "Can't think why you want one of these damned foreigners here cluttering up Christmas? Why can't we have him some other time? Can't stick foreigners! All right, all right, so Edwina Morecombe wished him on us. What's it got to do with her, I should like to know? Why doesn't she have him for Christmas?"

"Because you know very well," Mrs. Lacey had said, "that Edwina always goes to Claridge's."

Her husband had looked at her piercingly and said, "Not up to something, are you, Em?"

"Up to something?" said Em, opening very blue eyes. "Of course not. Why should I be?"

Old Colonel Lacey laughed, a deep, rumbling laugh. "I wouldn't put it past you, Em," he said. "When you look your most innocent is when you are up to something."

Revolving these things in her mind, Mrs. Lacey went on: "Edwina said she thought perhaps you might help us . . . I'm sure I don't know quite how, but she said that friends of yours had once found you very helpful in—in a case something like ours. I—well, perhaps you don't know what I'm talking about?"

Poirot looked at her encouragingly. Mrs. Lacey was close on seventy, as upright as a ramrod, with snow-white hair, pink cheeks, blue eyes, a ridiculous nose and a determined chin.

"If there is anything I can do I shall only be too happy to do it," said Poirot. "It is, I understand, a rather unfortunate matter of a young girl's infatuation."

Mrs. Lacey nodded. "Yes. It seems extraordinary that I should—well, want to talk to you about it. After all, you are a perfect stranger. . . ."

"And a foreigner," said Poirot, in an understanding manner.

"Yes," said Mrs. Lacey, "but perhaps that makes it easier, in a way. Anyhow, Edwina seemed to think that you might perhaps know something—how shall I put it—something useful about this young Desmond Lee-Wortley."

Poirot paused a moment to admire the ingenuity of Mr. Jesmond and the ease with which he had made use of Lady Morecombe to further his own purposes.

"He has not, I understand, a very good reputation, this young man?" he began delicately.

"No, indeed, he hasn't! A very bad reputation! But that's no help so far as Sarah is concerned. It's never any good, is it, telling young girls that men have a bad reputation? It—it just spurs them on!"

"You are so very right," said Poirot.

"In my young day," went on Mrs. Lacey. ("Oh dear, that's a very long time ago!) We used to be warned, you know, against certain young men, and of course it did heighten one's interest in them, and if one could possibly manage to dance with them, or to be alone with them in a dark conservatory—" she laughed. "That's why I wouldn't let Horace do any of the things he wanted to do."

"Tell me," said Poirot, "exactly what is it that troubles you?"

"Our son was killed in the war," said Mrs. Lacey. "My daughter-in-law died when Sarah was born so that she has always been with us, and we've brought her up. Perhaps we've brought her up unwisely—I don't know. But we thought we ought always to leave her as free as possible."

"That is desirable, I think," said Poirot. "One cannot go against the spirit of the times."

"No," said Mrs. Lacey, "that's just what I felt about it. And, of course, girls nowadays do these sort of things."

Poirot looked at her inquiringly.

"I think the way one expresses it," said Mrs. Lacey. "is that Sarah has got in with what they call the coffee-bar set. She won't go to dances or come out properly or be a deb or anything of that kind. Instead she has two rather unpleasant rooms in Chelsea down by the river and wears these funny clothes that they like to wear, and black stockings or bright green ones. Very thick stockings. (So prickly, I always think!) And she goes about without washing or combing her hair."

"Ça, c'est tout à fait naturelle," said Poirot. "It is the fashion of the moment. They grow out of it."

"Yes, I know," said Mrs. Lacey. "I wouldn't worry about that sort of thing. But you see she's taken up with this Desmond Lee-Wortley and he really has a very unsavoury reputation. He lives more or less on well-to-do girls. They seem to go quite mad about him. He very nearly married the Hope girl, but her people got her made a ward in court or something. And of course that's what Horace wants to do. He says he must do it for her protection. But I don't think it's really a good idea, M. Poirot. I mean, they'll just run away together and go to Scotland or Ireland or the Argentine or somewhere and either get married or else live together without getting married. And although it may be contempt of court and all that—well, it isn't really an answer, is it, in the end? Especially if a baby's coming. One has to give in then, and let them get married. And then, nearly always, it seems to me, after a year or two there's a divorce. And then the girl comes home and usually after a year or two she marries someone so nice he's almost dull and settles down. But it's particularly sad, it seems to me, if there is a child, because it's not the same thing, being brought up by a stepfather, however nice. No, I think it's much better if we did as we did in my young days. I mean the first young man one fell in love with was always someone undesirable. I remember I had a horrible passion for a young man called—now what was his name now?—how strange it is, I can't remember his Christian name at all! Tibbitt, that was his surname. Young Tibbitt. Of course, my father more or less forbade him the house, but he used to get asked to the same dances, and we used to dance together. And sometimes we'd escape and sit out together and occasionally friends would arrange picnics to which we both went. Of course, it was all very exciting and forbidden and one enjoyed it enormously. But one didn't go to the—well, to the lengths that girls go nowadays. And so, after a while, the Mr. Tibbitts faded out. And do you know, when I saw him four years later I was surprised what I could ever have seen in him! He seemed to be such a dull young man. Flashy, you know. No interesting conversation."

"One always thinks the days of one's own youth are best," said Poirot, somewhat sententiously.

"I know," said Mrs. Lacey. "It's tiresome, isn't it? I mustn't be tiresome. But all the same I don't want Sarah, who's a dear girl really, to marry Desmond Lee-Wortley. She and David Welwyn, who is staying here, were always such friends and so fond of each other, and we did hope, Horace and I, that they would grow up and marry. But of course she just finds him dull now, and she's absolutely infatuated with Desmond."

"I do not quite understand, Madame," said Poirot. "You have him here now, staying in the house, this Desmond Lee-Wortley?"

"That's my doing," said Mrs. Lacey. "Horace was all for forbidding her to see him and all that. Of course, in Horace's day, the father or guardian would have called round at the young man's lodgings with a horse whip! Horace was all for forbidding the fellow the house, and forbidding the girl to see him. I told him that was quite the wrong attitude to take. 'No,' I said. 'Ask him down here. We'll have him down for Christmas with the family party.' Of course, my husband said I was mad! But I said, 'At any rate, dear, let's try it. Let her see him in our atmosphere and our house and we'll be very nice to him and very polite, and perhaps then he'll seem less interesting to her'!"

"I think, as they say, you have something there, Madame," said Poirot. "I think your point of view is very wise. Wiser than your husband's."

"Well, I hope it is," said Mrs. Lacey doubtfully. "It doesn't seem to be working much yet. But of course he's only been here a couple of days." A sudden dimple showed in her wrinkled cheek. "I'll confess something to you, M. Poirot. I myself can't help liking him. I don't mean I really like him, with my mind, but I can feel the charm all right. Oh yes, I can see what Sarah sees in him. But I'm an old enough woman and have enough experience to know that he's absolutely no good. Even if I do enjoy his company. Though I do think," added Mrs. Lacey, rather wistfully, "he has some good points. He asked if he might bring his sister here, you know. She's had an operation and was in hospital. He said it was so sad for her being in a nursing home over Christmas and he wondered if it would be too much trouble if he could bring her with him. He said he'd take all her meals up to her and all that. Well now, I do think that was rather nice of him, don't you, M. Poirot?"

"It shows a consideration," said Poirot, thoughtfully, "which seems almost out of character."

"Oh, I don't know. You can have family affections at the same time as wishing to prey on a rich young girl. Sarah will be very rich, you know, not only with what we leave her—and of course that won't be very much because most of the money goes with the place to Colin, my grandson. But her mother was a very rich woman and Sarah will inherit all her money when she's twenty-one. She's only twenty now. No, I do think it was nice of Desmond to mind about his sister. And he didn't pretend she was anything very wonderful or that. She's a shorthand typist, I gather—does secretarial work in London. And he's been as good as his word and does carry up trays to her. Not all the time, of course, but quite often. So I think he has some nice points. But all the same," said Mrs. Lacey with great decision, "I don't want Sarah to marry him."

"From all I have heard and been told," said Poirot, "that would indeed be a disaster."

"Do you think it would be possible for you to help us in any way?" asked Mrs. Lacey.

"I think it is possible, yes," said Hercule Poirot, "but I do not wish to promise too much. For the Mr. Desmond Lee-Wortleys of this world are clever, Madame. But do not despair. One can, perhaps, do a little something. I shall at any rate, put forth my best endeavours, if only in gratitude for your kindness in asking me here for this Christmas festivity." He looked round him. "And it cannot be so easy these days to have Christmas festivities."

"No, indeed," Mrs. Lacey sighed. She leaned forward. "Do you know, M. Poirot, what I really dream of—what I would love to have?"

"But tell me, Madame."

"I simply long to have a small, modern bungalow. No, perhaps not a bungalow exactly, but a small, modern, easy-to-run house built somewhere in the park here, and live in it with an absolute up-to-date kitchen and no long passages. Everything easy and simple."

"It is a very practical idea, Madame."

"It's not practical for me," said Mrs. Lacey. "My husband adores this place. He loves living here. He doesn't mind being slightly uncomfortable, he doesn't mind the inconveniences and he would hate, simply hate, to live in a small modern house in the park!"

"So you sacrifice yourself to his wishes?"

Mrs. Lacey drew herself up. "I do not consider it a sacrifice, M. Poirot," she said. "I married my husband with the wish to make him happy. He has been a good husband to me and made me very happy all these years, and I wish to give happiness to him."

"So you will continue to live here," said Poirot.

"It's not really too uncomfortable," said Mrs. Lacey.

"No, no," said Poirot, hastily. "On the contrary, it is most comfortable. Your central heating and your bathwater are perfection."

"We spent a lot of money in making the house comfortable to live in," said Mrs. Lacey. "We were able to sell some land. Ripe for development, I think they call it. Fortunately right out of sight of the house on the other side of the park. Really rather an ugly bit of ground with no nice view, but we got a very good price for it. So that we have been able to have as many improvements as possible."

"But the service, Madame?"

"Oh, well, that presents less difficulty than you might think. Of course, one cannot expect to be looked after and waited upon as one used to be. Different people come in from the village. Two women in the morning, another two to cook lunch and wash it up, and different ones again in the evening. There are plenty of people who want to come and work for a few hours a day. Of course for Christmas we are very lucky. My dear Mrs. Ross always comes in every Christmas. She is a wonderful cook, really first-class. She retired about ten years ago, but she comes in to help us in any emergency. Then there is dear Peverell."

"Your butler?"

"Yes. He is pensioned off and lives in the little house near the lodge, but he is so devoted, and he insists on coming to wait on us at Christmas. Really, I'm terrified, M. Poirot, because he's so old and so shaky that I feel certain that if he carries anything heavy he will drop it. It's really an agony to watch him. And his heart is not good and I'm afraid of his doing too much. But it would hurt his feelings dreadfully if I did not let him come. He hems and hahs and makes disapproving noises when he sees the state our silver is in and within three days of being here, it is all wonderful again. Yes. He is a dear faithful friend." She smiled at Poirot. "So you see, we are all set for a happy Christmas. A white Christmas, too," she added as she looked out of the window. "See? It is beginning to snow. Ah, the children are coming in. You must meet them, M. Poirot."

Poirot was introduced with due ceremony. First, to Colin and Michael, the schoolboy grandson and his friend, nice polite lads of fifteen, one dark, one fair. Then to their cousin, Bridget, a black-haired girl of about the same age with enormous vitality.

"And this is my granddaughter, Sarah," said Mrs. Lacey.

Poirot looked with some interest at Sarah, an attractive girl with a mop of red hair, her manner seemed to him nervy and a trifle defiant, but she showed real affection for her grandmother.

"And this is Mr. Lee-Wortley."

Mr. Lee-Wortley wore a fisherman's jersey and tight black jeans; his hair was rather long and it seemed doubtful whether he had shaved that morning. In contrast to him was a young man introduced as David Welwyn, who was solid and quiet, with a pleasant smile, and rather obviously addicted to soap and water. There was one other member of the party, a handsome, rather intense-looking girl who was introduced as Diana Middleton.

Tea was brought in. A hearty meal of scones, crumpets, sandwiches and three kinds of cake. The younger members of the party appreciated the tea. Colonel Lacey came in last, remarking in a noncommittal voice:

                    The Missing Will & Other Stories

"Hey, tea? Oh yes, tea."

He received his cup of tea from his wife's hand, helped himself to two scones, cast a look of aversion at Desmond Lee-Wortley and sat down as far away from him as he could. He was a big man with bushy eyebrows and a red, weather-beaten face. He might have been taken for a farmer rather than the lord of the manor.

"Started to snow," he said. "It's going to be a white Christmas all right."

After tea the party dispersed.

"I expect they'll go and play with their tape recorders now," said Mrs. Lacey to Poirot. She looked indulgently after her grandson as he left the room. Her tone was that of one who says "The children are going to play with their toy soldiers."

"They're frightfully technical, of course," she said, "and very grand about it all."

The boys and Bridget, however, decided to go along to the lake and see if the ice on it was likely to make skating possible.

"I thought we could have skated on it this morning," said Colin. "But old Hodgkins said no. He's always so terribly careful."

"Come for a walk, David," said Diana Middleton, softly.

David hesitated for half a moment, his eyes on Sarah's red head. She was standing by Desmond Lee-Wortley, her hand on his arm, looking up into his face.

"All right," said David Welwyn, "yes, let's."

Diana slipped a quick hand through his arm and they turned towards the door into the garden. Sarah said:

"Shall we go, too, Desmond? It's fearfully stuffy in the house."

"Who wants to walk?" said Desmond. "I'll get my car out. We'll go along to the Speckled Boar and have a drink."

Sarah hesitated for a moment before saying:

"Let's go to Market Ledbury to the White Hart. It's much more fun."

Though for all the world she would not have put it into words, Sarah had an instinctive revulsion from going down to the local pub with Desmond. It was, somehow, not in the tradition of Kings Lacey. The women of Kings Lacey had never frequented the bar of the Speckled Boar. She had an obscure feeling that to go there would be to let old Colonel Lacey and his wife down. And why not? Desmond Lee-Wortley would have said. For a moment of exasperation Sarah felt that he ought to know why not! One didn't upset such old darlings as Grandfather and dear old Em unless it was necessary. They'd been very sweet, really, letting her lead her own life, not understanding in the least why she wanted to live in Chelsea in the way she did, but accepting it. That was due to Em of course. Grandfather would have kicked up no end of a row.

Sarah had no illusions about her grandfather's attitude. It was not his doing that Desmond had been asked to stay at Kings Lacey. That was Em, and Em was a darling and always had been.

When Desmond had gone to fetch his car, Sarah popped her head into the drawing room again.

"We're going over to Market Ledbury," she said. "We thought we'd have a drink there at the White Hart."

There was a slight amount of defiance in her voice, but Mrs. Lacey did not seem to notice it.

"Well, dear," she said. "I'm sure that will be very nice. David and Diana have gone for a walk, I see. I'm so glad. I really think it was a brainwave on my part to ask Diana here. So sad being left a widow so young—only twenty-two—I do hope she marries again soon."

Sarah looked at her sharply. "What are you up to, Em?"

"It's my little plan," said Mrs. Lacey gleefully. "I think she's just right for David. Of course I know he was terribly in love with you, Sarah dear, but you'd no use for him and I realize that he isn't your type. But I don't want him to go on being unhappy, and I think Diana will really suit him."

 The Missing Will & Other Stories

"What a matchmaker you are, Em," said Sarah.

"I know," said Mrs. Lacey. "Old women always are. Diana's quite keen on him already, I think. Don't you think she'd be just right for him?"

"I shouldn't say so," said Sarah. "I think Diana's far too—well, too intense, too serious. I should think David would find it terribly boring being married to her."

"Well, we'll see," said Mrs. Lacey. "Anyway, you don't want him, do you, dear?"

"No, indeed," said Sarah, very quickly. She added, in a sudden rush, "You do like Desmond, don't you, Em?"

"I'm sure he's very nice indeed," said Mrs. Lacey.

"Grandfather doesn't like him," said Sarah.

"Well, you could hardly expect him to, could you?" said Mrs. Lacey reasonably, "but I dare say he'll come round when he gets used to the idea. You mustn't rush him, Sarah dear. Old people are very slow to change their minds and your grandfather is rather obstinate."

"I don't care what Grandfather thinks or says," said Sarah. "I shall get married to Desmond whenever I like!"

"I know, dear, I know. But do try and be realistic about it. Your grandfather could cause a lot of trouble, you know. You're not of age yet. In another year you can do as you please. I expect Horace will have come round long before that."

"You're on my side aren't you, darling?" said Sarah. She flung her arms round her grandmother's neck and gave her an affectionate kiss.

"I want you to be happy," said Mrs. Lacey. "Ah! there's your young man bringing his car round. You know, I like these very tight trousers these young men wear nowadays. They look so smart—only, of course, it does accentuate knock knees."

Yes, Sarah thought, Desmond had got knock knees, she had never noticed it before. . . .

"Go on, dear, enjoy yourself," said Mrs. Lacey.

She watched her go out to the car, then, remembering her foreign guest, she went along to the library. Looking in, however, she saw that Hercule Poirot was taking a pleasant little nap, and smiling to herself, she went across the hall and out into the kitchen to have a conference with Mrs. Ross.

"Come on, beautiful," said Desmond. "Your family cutting up rough because you're coming out to a pub? Years behind the times here, aren't they?"

"Of course they're not making a fuss," said Sarah, sharply as she got into the car.

"What's the idea of having that foreign fellow down? He's a detective, isn't he? What needs detecting here?"

"Oh, he's not here professionally," said Sarah. "Edwina Morecombe, my grandmother, asked us to have him. I think he's retired from professional work long ago."

"Sounds like a broken-down old cab horse," said Desmond.

"He wanted to see an old-fashioned English Christmas, I believe," said Sarah vaguely.

Desmond laughed scornfully. "Such a lot of tripe, that sort of thing," he said. "How you can stand it I don't know."

Sarah's red hair was tossed back and her aggressive chin shot up.

"I enjoy it!" she said defiantly.

"You can't, baby. Let's cut the whole thing tomorrow. Go over to Scarborough or somewhere."

"I couldn't possibly do that."

"Why not?"

"Oh, it would hurt their feelings."

"Oh, bilge! You know you don't enjoy this childish sentimental bosh."

"Well, not really perhaps but—" Sarah broke off. She realized with a feeling of guilt that she was looking forward a good deal to the Christmas celebration. She enjoyed the whole thing, but she was ashamed to admit that to Desmond. It was not the thing to enjoy Christmas and family life. Just for a moment she wished that Desmond had not come down here at Christmastime. In fact, she almost wished that Desmond had not come down here at all. It was much more fun seeing Desmond in London than here at home.

In the meantime the boys and Bridget were walking back from the lake, still discussing earnestly the problems of skating. Flecks of snow had been falling, and looking up at the sky it could be prophesied that before long there was going to be a heavy snowfall.

"It's going to snow all night," said Colin. "Bet you by Christmas morning we have a couple of feet of snow."

The prospect was a pleasurable one.

"Let's make a snowman," said Michael.

"Good lord," said Colin, "I haven't made a snowman since—well, since I was about four years old."

"I don't believe it's a bit easy to do," said Bridget. "I mean, you have to know how."

"We might make an effigy of M. Poirot," said Colin. "Give it a big black moustache. There is one in the dressing-up box."

"I don't see, you know," said Michael thoughtfully, "how M. Poirot could ever have been a detective. I don't see how he'd ever be able to disguise himself."

"I know," said Bridget, "and one can't imagine him running about with a microscope and looking for clues or measuring footprints."

"I've got an idea," said Colin. "Let's put on a show for him!"

"What do you mean, a show?" asked Bridget.

"Well, arrange a murder for him."

"What a gorgeous idea," said Bridget. "Do you mean a body in the snow—that sort of thing?"

"Yes. It would make him feel at home, wouldn't it?"

Bridget giggled.

"I don't know that I'd go as far as that."

"If it snows," said Colin, "we'll have the perfect setting. A body and footprints—we'll have to think that out rather carefully and pinch one of Grandfather's daggers and make some blood."

They came to a halt and oblivious to the rapidly falling snow, entered into an excited discussion.

"There's a paintbox in the old schoolroom. We could mix up some blood—crimson-lake, I should think."

"Crimson-lake's a bit too pink, I think," said Bridget. "It ought to be a bit browner."

"Who's going to be the body?" asked Michael.

"I'll be the body," said Bridget quickly.

"Oh, look here," said Colin, "I thought of it."

"Oh, no, no," said Bridget, "it must be me. It's got to be a girl. It's more exciting. Beautiful girl lying lifeless in the snow."

"Beautiful girl! Ah-ha," said Michael in derision.

"I've got black hair, too," said Bridget.

"What's that got to do with it?"

"Well, it'll show up so well on the snow and I shall wear my red pyjamas."

"If you wear red pyjamas, they won't show the bloodstains," said Michael in a practical manner.

"But they'd look so effective against the snow," said Bridget, "and they've got white facings, you know, so the blood could be on that. Oh, won't it be gorgeous? Do you think he will really be taken in?"

 The Missing Will & Other Stories

"He will if we do it well enough," said Michael. "We'll have just your footprints in the snow and one other person's going to the body and coming away from it—a man's, of course. He won't want to disturb them, so he won't know that you're not really dead. You don't think," Michael stopped, struck by a sudden idea. The others looked at him. "You don't think he'll be annoyed about it?"

"Oh, I shouldn't think so," said Bridget, with facile optimism. "I'm sure he'll understand that we've just done it to entertain him. A sort of Christmas treat."

"I don't think we ought to do it on Christmas Day," said Colin reflectively. "I don't think Grandfather would like that very much."

"Boxing Day then," said Bridget.

"Boxing Day would be just right," said Michael.

"And it'll give us more time, too," pursued Bridget. "After all, there are a lot of things to arrange. Let's go and have a look at all the props."

They hurried into the house.

The evening was a busy one. Holly and mistletoe had been brought in in large quantities and a Christmas tree had been set up at one end of the dining room. Everyone helped to decorate it, to put up the branches of holly behind pictures and to hang mistletoe in a convenient position in the hall.

"I had no idea anything so archaic still went on," murmured Desmond to Sarah with a sneer.

"We've always done it," said Sarah, defensively.

"What a reason!"

"Oh, don't be tiresome, Desmond. I think it's fun."

"Sarah my sweet, you can't!"

"Well, not—not really perhaps but—I do in a way."

"Who's going to brave the snow and go to midnight mass?" asked Mrs. Lacey at twenty minutes to twelve.

"Not me," said Desmond. "Come on, Sarah."

With a hand on her arm he guided her into the library and went over to the record case.

"There are limits, darling," said Desmond. "Midnight mass!"

"Yes," said Sarah. "Oh yes."

With a good deal of laughter, donning of coats and stamping of feet, most of the others got off. The two boys, Bridget, David and Diana set out for the ten minutes' walk to the church through the falling snow. Their laughter died away in the distance.

"Midnight mass!" said Colonel Lacey, snorting. "Never went to midnight mass in my young days. Mass, indeed! Popish, that is! Oh, I beg your pardon, M. Poirot."

Poirot waved a hand. "It is quite all right. Do not mind me."

"Matins is good enough for anybody, I should say," said the colonel. "Proper Sunday morning service. 'Hark the herald angels sing,' and all the good old Christmas hymns. And then back to Christmas dinner. That's right, isn't it, Em?"

"Yes, dear," said Mrs. Lacey. "That's what we do. But the young ones enjoy the midnight service. And it's nice, really, that they want to go."

"Sarah and that fellow don't want to go."

"Well, there dear, I think you're wrong," said Mrs. Lacey. "Sarah, you know, did want to go, but she didn't like to say so."

"Beats me why she cares what that fellow's opinion is."

"She's very young, really," said Mrs. Lacey placidly. "Are you going to bed, M. Poirot? Good night. I hope you'll sleep well."

"And you, Madame? Are you not going to bed yet?"

"Not just yet," said Mrs. Lacey. "I've got the stockings to fill, you see. Oh, I know they're all practically grown up, but they do like their stockings. One puts jokes in them! Silly little things. But it all makes for a lot of fun."

"You work very hard to make this a happy house at Christmas time," said Poirot. "I honour you."

He raised her hand to his lips in a courtly fashion.

"Hm," grunted Colonel Lacey, as Poirot departed. "Flowery sort of fellow. Still—he appreciates you."

Mrs. Lacey dimpled up at him. "Have you noticed, Horace, that I'm standing under the mistletoe?" she asked with the demureness of a girl of nineteen.

Hercule Poirot entered his bedroom. It was a large room well provided with radiators. As he went over towards the big four-poster bed he noticed an envelope lying on his pillow. He opened it and drew out a piece of paper. On it was a shakily printed message in capital letters.

DON'T EAT NONE OF THE PLUM PUDDING. ONE AS WISHES YOU WELL.

Hercule Poirot stared at it. His eyebrows rose. "Cryptic," he murmured, "and most unexpected."

Christmas dinner took place at 2 p.m. and was a feast indeed. Enormous logs crackled merrily in the wide fireplace and above their crackling rose the babel of many tongues talking together. Oyster soup had been consumed, two enormous turkeys had come and gone, mere carcasses of their former selves. Now, the supreme moment, the Christmas pudding was brought in, in state! Old Peverell, his hands and his knees shaking with the weakness of eighty years, permitted no one but himself to bear it in. Mrs. Lacey sat, her hands pressed together in nervous apprehension. One Christmas, she felt sure, Peverell would fall down dead. Having either to take the risk of letting him fall down dead or of hurting his feelings to such an extent that he would probably prefer to be dead than alive, she had so far chosen the former alternative. On a silver dish the Christmas pudding reposed in its glory. A large football of a pudding, a piece of holly stuck in it like a triumphant flag and glorious flames of blue and red rising round it. There was a cheer and cries of "Ooh-ah."

One thing Mrs. Lacey had done: prevailed upon Peverell to place the pudding in front of her so that she could help it rather than hand it in turn round the table. She breathed a sigh of relief as it was deposited safely in front of her. Rapidly the plates were passed round, flames still licking the portions.

"Wish, M. Poirot," cried Bridget. "Wish before the flame goes. Quick, Gran darling, quick."

Mrs. Lacey leant back with a sigh of satisfaction. Operation Pudding had been a success. In front of everyone was a helping with flames still licking it. There was a momentary silence all round the table as everyone wished hard.

There was nobody to notice the rather curious expression on the face of M. Poirot as he surveyed the portion of pudding on his plate. "Don't eat none of the plum pudding." What on earth did that sinister warning mean? There could be nothing different about his portion of plum pudding from that of everyone else! Sighing as he admitted himself baffled—and Hercule Poirot never liked to admit himself baffled—he picked up his spoon and fork.

"Hard sauce, M. Poirot?"

Poirot helped himself appreciatively to hard sauce.

"Swiped my best brandy again, eh Em?" said the colonel good-humouredly from the other end of the table. Mrs. Lacey twinkled at him.

"Mrs. Ross insists on having the best brandy, dear," she said. "She says it makes all the difference."

"Well, well," said Colonel Lacey, "Christmas comes but once a year and Mrs. Ross is a great woman. A great woman and a great cook."

"She is indeed," said Colin. "Smashing plum pudding, this. Mmmm." He filled an appreciative mouth.

Gently, almost gingerly, Hercule Poirot attacked his portion of pudding. He ate a mouthful. It was delicious! He ate another.

Something tinkled faintly on his plate. He investigated with a fork. Bridget, on his left, came to his aid.

"You've got something, M. Poirot," she said. "I wonder what it is."

Poirot detached a little silver object from the surrounding raisins that clung to it.

"Oooh," said Bridget, "it's the bachelor's button! M. Poirot's got the bachelor's button!"

Hercule Poirot dipped the small silver button into the finger-glass of water that stood by his plate, and washed it clear of pudding crumbs.

"It is very pretty," he observed.

"That means you're going to be a bachelor, M. Poirot," explained Colin helpfully.

"That is to be expected," said Poirot gravely. "I have been a bachelor for many long years and it is unlikely that I shall change that status now."

"Oh, never say die," said Michael. "I saw in the paper that someone of ninety-five married a girl of twenty-two the other day."

"You encourage me," said Hercule Poirot.

Colonel Lacey uttered a sudden exclamation. His face became purple and his hand went to his mouth.

"Confound it, Emmeline," he roared, "why on earth do you let the cook put glass in the pudding?"

"Glass!" cried Mrs. Lacey, astonished.

Colonel Lacey withdrew the offending substance from his mouth. "Might have broken a tooth," he grumbled. "Or swallowed the damn thing and had appendicitis."

He dropped the piece of glass into the finger bowl, rinsed it and held it up.

"God bless my soul," he ejaculated. "It's a red stone out of one of the cracker brooches." He held it aloft.

"You permit?"

Very deftly M. Poirot stretched across his neighbour, took it from Colonel Lacey's fingers and examined it attentively. As the squire had said, it was an enormous red stone the colour of a ruby. The light gleamed from its facets as he turned it about. Somewhere around the table a chair was pushed sharply back and then drawn in again.

"Phew!" cried Michael. "How wizard it would be if it was real."

"Perhaps it is real," said Bridget hopefully.

"Oh, don't be an ass, Bridget. Why a ruby of that size would be worth thousands and thousands and thousands of pounds. Wouldn't it, M. Poirot?"

"It would indeed," said Poirot.

"But what I can't understand," said Mrs. Lacey, "is how it got into the pudding."

"Oooh," said Colin, diverted by his last mouthful, "I've got the pig. It isn't fair."

Bridget chanted immediately, "Colin's got the pig! Colin's got the pig! Colin is the greedy guzzling pig!"

"I've got the ring," said Diana in a clear, high voice.

"Good for you, Diana. You'll be married first, of us all."

"I've got the thimble," wailed Bridget.

"Bridget's going to be an old maid," chanted the two boys. "Yah, Bridget's going to be an old maid."

"Who's got the money?" demanded David. "There's a real ten shilling piece, gold, in this pudding. I know. Mrs. Ross told me so."

"I think I'm the lucky one," said Desmond Lee-Wortley.

Colonel Lacey's two next door neighbours heard him mutter. "Yes, you would be."

"I've got a ring, too," said David. He looked across at Diana. "Quite a coincidence, isn't it?"

The laughter went on. Nobody noticed that M. Poirot carelessly, as though thinking of something else, had dropped the red stone into his pocket.

Mince pies and Christmas dessert followed the pudding. The older members of the party then retired for a welcome siesta before the teatime ceremony of the lighting of the Christmas tree. Hercule Poirot, however, did not take a siesta. Instead, he made his way to the enormous old-fashioned kitchen.

"It is permitted," he asked, looking round and beaming, "that I congratulate the cook on this marvellous meal that I have just eaten?"

There was a moment's pause and then Mrs. Ross came forward in a stately manner to meet him. She was a large woman, nobly built with all the dignity of a stage duchess. Two lean grey-haired women were beyond in the scullery washing up and a tow-haired girl was moving to and fro between the scullery and the kitchen. But these were obviously mere myrmidons. Mrs. Ross was the queen of the kitchen quarters.

"I am glad to hear you enjoyed it, sir," she said graciously.

"Enjoyed it!" cried Hercule Poirot. With an extravagant foreign gesture he raised his hand to his lips, kissed it, and wafted the kiss to the ceiling. "But you are a genius, Mrs. Ross! A genius! Never have I tasted such a wonderful meal. The oyster soup—" he made an expressive noise with his lips "—and the stuffing. The chestnut stuffing in the turkey, that was quite unique in my experience."

"Well, it's funny that you should say that, sir," said Mrs. Ross graciously. "It's a very special recipe, that stuffing. It was given me by an Austrian chef that I worked with many years ago. But all the rest," she added, "is just good, plain English cooking."

"And is there anything better?" demanded Hercule Poirot.

"Well, it's nice of you to say so, sir. Of course, you being a foreign gentleman might have preferred the continental style. Not but what I can't manage continental dishes too."

"I am sure, Mrs. Ross, you could manage anything! But you must know that English cooking—good English cooking, not the cooking one gets in the second-class hotels or the restaurants—is much appreciated by gourmets on the continent, and I believe I am correct in saying that a special expedition was made to London in the early eighteen hundreds, and a report sent back to France of the wonders of the English puddings. 'We have nothing like that in France,' they wrote. 'It is worth making a journey to London just to taste the varieties and excellencies of the English puddings.' And above all puddings," continued Poirot, well launched now on a kind of rhapsody, "is the Christmas plum pudding, such as we have eaten today. That was a homemade pudding, was it not? Not a bought one?"

"Yes, indeed, sir. Of my own making and my own recipe such as I've made for many years. When I came here Mrs. Lacey said that she'd ordered a pudding from a London store to save me the trouble. But no, Madam, I said, that may be kind of you but no bought pudding from a store can equal a homemade Christmas one. Mind you," said Mrs. Ross, warming to her subject like the artist she was, "it was made too soon before the day. A good Christmas pudding should be made some weeks before and allowed to wait. The longer they're kept, within reason, the better they are. I mind now that when I was a child and we went to church every Sunday, we'd start listening for the collect that begins 'Stir up O Lord we beseech thee' because that collect was the signal, as it were, that the puddings should be made that week. And so they always were. We had the collect on the Sunday, and that week sure enough my mother would make the Christmas puddings. And so it should have been here this year. As it was, that pudding was only made three days ago, the day before you arrived, sir. However, I kept to the old custom. Everyone in the house had to come out into the kitchen and have a stir and make a wish. That's an old custom, sir, and I've always held to it."

"Most interesting," said Hercule Poirot. "Most interesting. And so everyone came out into the kitchen?"

"Yes, sir. The young gentlemen, Miss Bridget and the London gentleman who's staying here, and his sister and Mr. David and Miss Diana—Mrs. Middleton, I should say—All had a stir, they did."

"How many puddings did you make? Is this the only one?"

"No, sir, I made four. Two large ones and two smaller ones. The other large one I planned to serve on New Year's Day and the smaller ones were for Colonel and Mrs. Lacey when they're alone like and not so many in the family."

"I see, I see," said Poirot.

"As a matter of fact, sir," said Mrs. Ross, "it was the wrong pudding you had for lunch today."

"The wrong pudding?" Poirot frowned. "How is that?"

"Well, sir, we have a big Christmas mould. A china mould with a pattern of holly and mistletoe on top and we always have the Christmas Day pudding boiled in that. But there was a most unfortunate accident. This morning, when Annie was getting it down from the shelf in the larder, she slipped and dropped it and it broke. Well, sir, naturally I couldn't serve that, could I? There might have been splinters in it. So we had to use the other one—the New Year's Day one, which was in a plain bowl. It makes a nice round but it's not so decorative as the Christmas mould. Really, where we'll get another mould like that I don't know. They don't make things in that size nowadays. All tiddly bits of things. Why, you can't even buy a breakfast dish that'll take a proper eight to ten eggs and bacon. Ah, things aren't what they were."

"No, indeed," said Poirot. "But today that is not so. This Christmas Day has been like the Christmas Days of old, is that not true?"

Mrs. Ross sighed. "Well, I'm glad you say so, sir, but of course I haven't the help now that I used to have. Not skilled help, that is. The girls nowadays—" she lowered her voice slightly, "—they mean very well and they're very willing but they've not been trained, sir, if you understand what I mean."

"Times change, yes," said Hercule Poirot. "I too find it sad sometimes."

"This house, sir," said Mrs. Ross, "it's too large, you know, for the mistress and the colonel. The mistress, she knows that. Living in a corner of it as they do, it's not the same thing at all. It only comes alive, as you might say, at Christmas time when all the family come."

"It is the first time, I think, that Mr. Lee-Wortley and his sister have been here?"

"Yes, sir." A note of slight reserve crept into Mrs. Ross's voice. "A very nice gentleman he is but, well—it seems a funny friend for Miss Sarah to have, according to our ideas. But there—London ways are different! It's sad that his sister's so poorly. Had an operation, she had. She seemed all right the first day she was here, but that very day, after we'd been stirring the puddings, she was took bad again and she's been in bed ever since. Got up too soon after her operation, I expect. Ah, doctors nowadays, they have you out of hospital before you can hardly stand on your feet. Why, my very own nephew's wife . . ." And Mrs. Ross went into a long and spirited tale of hospital treatment as accorded to her relations, comparing it unfavourably with the consideration that had been lavished upon them in older times.

Poirot duly commiserated with her. "It remains," he said, "to thank you for this exquisite and sumptuous meal. You permit a little acknowledgement of my appreciation?" A crisp five pound note passed from his hand into that of Mrs. Ross who said perfunctorily:

"You really shouldn't do that, sir."

"I insist. I insist."

"Well, it's very kind of you indeed, sir." Mrs. Ross accepted the tribute as no more than her due. "And I wish you, sir, a very happy Christmas and a prosperous New Year."

The end of Christmas Day was like the end of most Christmas Days. The tree was lighted, a splendid Christmas cake came in for tea, was greeted with approval but was partaken of only moderately. There was cold supper.

Both Poirot and his host and hostess went to bed early.

"Good night, M. Poirot," said Mrs. Lacey. "I hope you've enjoyed yourself."

"It has been a wonderful day, Madame, wonderful."

"You're looking very thoughtful," said Mrs. Lacey.

"It is the English pudding that I consider."

"You found it a little heavy, perhaps?" asked Mrs. Lacey delicately.

"No, no, I do not speak gastronomically. I consider its significance."

"It's traditional, of course," said Mrs. Lacey. "Well, good night, M. Poirot, and don't dream too much of Christmas puddings and mince pies."

"Yes," murmured Poirot to himself as he undressed. "It is a problem certainly, that Christmas plum pudding. There is here something that I do not understand at all." He shook his head in a vexed manner. "Well—we shall see."

After making certain preparations, Poirot went to bed, but not to sleep.

It was some two hours later that his patience was rewarded. The door of his bedroom opened very gently. He smiled to himself. It was as he had thought it would be. His mind went back fleetingly to the cup of coffee so politely handed him by Desmond Lee-Wortley. A little later, when Desmond's back was turned, he had laid the cup down for a few moments on a table. He had then apparently picked it up again and Desmond had had the satisfaction, if satisfaction it was, of seeing him drink the coffee to the last drop. But a little smile lifted Poirot's moustache as he reflected that it was not he but someone else who was sleeping a good sound sleep tonight.

"That pleasant young David," said Poirot to himself, "he is worried, unhappy. It will do him no harm to have a night's really sound sleep. And now, let us see what will happen?"

He lay quite still, breathing in an even manner with occasionally a suggestion, but the very faintest suggestion, of a snore.

Someone came up to the bed and bent over him. Then, satisfied, that someone turned away and went to the dressing table. By the light of a tiny torch the visitor was examining Poirot's belongings neatly arranged on top of the dressing table. Fingers explored the wallet, gently pulled open the drawers of the dressing table, then extended the search to the pockets of Poirot's clothes. Finally the visitor approached the bed and with great caution slid his hand under the pillow. Withdrawing his hand, he stood for a moment or two as though uncertain what to do next. He walked round the room looking inside ornaments, went into the adjoining bathroom from whence he presently returned. Then, with a faint exclamation of disgust, he went out of the room.

"Ah," said Poirot, under his breath. "You have a disappointment. Yes, yes, a serious disappointment. Bah! To imagine, even, that Hercule Poirot would hide something where you could find it!" Then, turning over on his other side, he went peacefully to sleep.

He was aroused next morning by an urgent soft tapping on his door.

"Qui est lá? Come in, come in."

The door opened. Breathless, red-faced, Colin stood upon the threshold. Behind him stood Michael.

"Monsieur Poirot, Monsieur Poirot."

"But yes?" Poirot sat up in bed. "It is the early tea? But no. It is you, Colin. What has occurred?"

Colin was, for a moment, speechless. He seemed to be under the grip of some strong emotion. In actual fact it was the sight of the nightcap that Hercule Poirot wore that affected for the moment his organs of speech. Presently he controlled himself and spoke.

"I think—M. Poirot, could you help us? Something rather awful has happened."

"Something has happened? But what?"

"It's—it's Bridget. She's out there in the snow. I think—she doesn't move or speak and—oh, you'd better come and look for yourself. I'm terribly afraid—she may be dead."

"What?" Poirot cast aside his bed covers. "Mademoiselle Bridget—dead!"

"I think—I think somebody's killed her. There's—there's blood and—oh do come!"

"But certainly. But certainly. I come on the instant."

With great practicality Poirot inserted his feet into his outdoor shoes and pulled a fur-lined overcoat over his pyjamas.

"I come," he said. "I come on the moment. You have aroused the house?"

"No. No, so far I haven't told anyone but you. I thought it would be better. Grandfather and Gran aren't up yet. They're laying breakfast downstairs, but I didn't say anything to Peverell. She— Bridget—she's round the other side of the house, near the terrace and the library window."

"I see. Lead the way. I will follow."

Turning away to hide his delighted grin, Colin led the way downstairs. They went out through the side door. It was a clear morning with the sun not yet high over the horizon. It was not snowing now, but it had snowed heavily during the night and everywhere around was an unbroken carpet of thick snow. The world looked very pure and white and beautiful.

"There!" said Colin breathlessly. "I—it's—there!" He pointed dramatically.

The scene was indeed dramatic enough. A few yards away Bridget lay in the snow. She was wearing scarlet pyjamas and a white wool wrap thrown round her shoulders. The white wool wrap was stained with crimson. Her head was turned aside and hidden by the mass of her outspread black hair. One arm was under her body, the other lay flung out, the fingers clenched, and standing up in the centre of the crimson stain was the hilt of a large curved Kurdish knife which Colonel Lacey had shown to his guests only the evening before.

"Mon Dieu!" ejaculated M. Poirot. "It is like something on the stage!"

There was a faint choking noise from Michael. Colin thrust himself quickly into the breach.

"I know," he said. "It—it doesn't seem real somehow, does it. Do you see those footprints—I suppose we mustn't disturb them?"

"Ah yes, the footprints. No, we must be careful not to disturb those footprints."

"That's what I thought," said Colin. "That's why I wouldn't let anyone go near her until we got you. I thought you'd know what to do."

"All the same," said Hercule Poirot briskly, "first, we must see if she is still alive? Is not that so?"

"Well—yes—of course," said Michael, a little doubtfully, "but you see, we thought—I mean, we didn't like—"

"Ah, you have the prudence! You have read the detective stories. It is most important that nothing should be touched and that the body should be left as it is. But we cannot be sure as yet if it is a body, can we? After all, though prudence is admirable, common humanity comes first. We must think of the doctor, must we not, before we think of the police?"

"Oh yes. Of course," said Colin, still a little taken aback.

"We only thought—I mean—we thought we'd better get you before we did anything," said Michael hastily.

"Then you will both remain here," said Poirot. "I will approach from the other side so as not to disturb these footprints. Such excellent footprints, are they not—so very clear? The footprints of a man and a girl going out together to the place where she lies. And then the man's footsteps come back but the girl's—do not."

"They must be the footprints of the murderer," said Colin, with bated breath.

"Exactly," said Poirot. "The footprints of the murderer. A long narrow foot with rather a peculiar type of shoe. Very interesting. Easy, I think, to recognize. Yes, those footprints will be very important."

At that moment Desmond Lee-Wortley came out of the house with Sarah and joined them.

"What on earth are you all doing here?" he demanded in a somewhat theatrical manner. "I saw you from my bedroom window. What's up? Good lord, what's this? It—it looks like—"

"Exactly," said Hercule Poirot. "It looks like murder, does it not?"

Sarah gave a gasp, then shot a quick suspicious glance at the two boys.

"You mean someone's killed the girl—what's-her-name—Bridget?" demanded Desmond. "Who on earth would want to kill her? It's unbelievable!"

"There are many things that are unbelievable," said Poirot. "Especially before breakfast, is it not? That is what one of your classics says. Six impossible things before breakfast." He added: "Please wait here, all of you."

Carefully making a circuit, he approached Bridget and bent for a moment down over the body. Colin and Michael were now both shaking with suppressed laughter. Sarah joined them, murmuring "What have you two been up to?"

"Good old Bridget," whispered Colin. "Isn't she wonderful? Not a twitch!"

"I've never seen anything look so dead as Bridget does," whispered Michael.

Hercule Poirot straightened up again.

"This is a terrible thing," he said. His voice held an emotion it had not held before.

Overcome by mirth, Michael and Colin both turned away. In a choked voice Michael said:

"What—what must we do?"

"There is only one thing to do," said Poirot. "We must send for the police. Will one of you telephone or would you prefer me to do it?"

"I think," said Colin, "I think—what about it, Michael?"

"Yes," said Michael, "I think the jig's up now." He stepped forward. For the first time he seemed a little unsure of himself. "I'm awfully sorry," he said, "I hope you won't mind too much. It—er—it was a sort of joke for Christmas and all that, you know. We thought we'd—well, lay on a murder for you."

"You thought you would lay on a murder for me? Then this—then this—"

"It's just a show we put on," explained. Colin, "to—to make you feel at home, you know."

"Aha," said Hercule Poirot. "I understand. You make of me the April fool, is that it? But today is not April the first, it is December the twenty-sixth."

"I suppose we oughtn't to have done it really," said Colin, "but—but—you don't mind very much, do you, M. Poirot? Come on, Bridget," he called, "get up. You must be half frozen to death already."

The figure in the snow, however, did not stir.

"It is odd," said Hercule Poirot, "she does not seem to hear you." He looked thoughtfully at them. "It is a joke, you say? You are sure this is a joke?"

"Why, yes." Colin spoke uncomfortably. "We—we didn't mean any harm."

"But why then does Mademoiselle Bridget not get up?"

"I can't imagine," said Colin.

"Come on, Bridget," said Sarah impatiently. "Don't go on lying there playing the fool."

"We really are very sorry, M. Poirot," said Colin apprehensively. "We do really apologize."

"You need not apologize," said Poirot, in a peculiar tone.

"What do you mean?" Colin stared at him. He turned again. "Bridget! Bridget! What's the matter? Why doesn't she get up? Why does she go on lying there?"

Poirot beckoned to Desmond. "You, Mr. Lee-Wortley. Come here—"

Desmond joined him.

"Feel her pulse," said Poirot.

Desmond Lee-Wortley bent down. He touched the arm—the wrist.

"There's no pulse . . ." he stared at Poirot. "Her arm's still. Good God, she really is dead!"

Poirot nodded. "Yes, she is dead," he said. "Someone has turned the comedy into a tragedy."

"Someone—who?"

"There is a set of footprints going and returning. A set of footprints that bears a strong resemblance to the footprints you have just made, Mr. Lee-Wortley, coming from the path to this spot."

Desmond Lee-Wortley wheeled round.

"What on earth—Are you accusing me? ME? You're crazy! Why on earth should I want to kill the girl?"

"Ah—why? I wonder . . . Let us see. . . ."

He bent down and very gently prised open the stiff fingers of the girl's clenched hand.

Desmond drew a sharp breath. He gazed down unbelievingly. In the palm of the dead girl's hand was what appeared to be a large ruby.

"It's that damn thing out of the pudding!" he cried.

"Is it?" said Poirot. "Are you sure?"

"Of course it is."

With a swift movement Desmond bent down and plucked the red stone out of Bridget's hand.

"You should not do that," said Poirot reproachfully. "Nothing should have been disturbed."

"I haven't disturbed the body, have I? But this thing might—might get lost and it's evidence. The great thing is to get the police here as soon as possible. I'll go at once and telephone."

He wheeled round and ran sharply towards the house. Sarah came swiftly to Poirot's side.

"I don't understand," she whispered. Her face was dead white. "I don't understand." She caught at Poirot's arm. "What did you mean about—about the footprints?"

"Look for yourself, Mademoiselle."

The footprints that led to the body and back again were the same as the ones just made accompanying Poirot to the girl's body and back.

"You mean—that it was Desmond? Nonsense!"

Suddenly the noise of a car came through the clear air. They wheeled round. They saw the car clearly enough driving at a furious pace down the drive and Sarah recognized what car it was.

"It's Desmond," she said. "It's Desmond's car. He—he must have gone to fetch the police instead of telephoning."

Diana Middleton came running out of the house to join them.

"What's happened?" she cried in a breathless voice. "Desmond just came rushing into the house. He said something about Bridget being killed and then he rattled the telephone but it was dead. He couldn't get an answer. He said the wires must have been cut. He said the only thing was to take a car and go for the police. Why the police? . . ."

Poirot made a gesture.

"Bridget?" Diana stared at him. "But surely—isn't it a joke of some kind? I heard something—something last night. I thought that they were going to play a joke on you, M. Poirot?"

"Yes," said Poirot, "that was the idea—to play a joke on me. But now come into the house, all of you. We shall catch our deaths of cold here and there is nothing to be done until Mr. Lee-Wortley returns with the police."

"But look here," said Colin, "we can't—we can't leave Bridget here alone."

"You can do her no good by remaining," said Poirot gently. "Come, it is a sad, a very sad tragedy, but there is nothing we can do anymore to help Mademoiselle Bridget. So let us come in and get warm and have perhaps a cup of tea or of coffee."

They followed him obediently into the house. Peverell was just about to strike the gong. If he thought it extraordinary for most of the household to be outside and for Poirot to make an appearance in pyjamas and an overcoat, he displayed no sign of it. Peverell in his old age was still the perfect butler. He noticed nothing that he was not asked to notice. They went into the dining room and sat down. When they all had a cup of coffee in front of them and were sipping it, Poirot spoke.

"I have to recount to you," he said, "a little history. I cannot tell you all the details, no. But I can give you the main outline. It concerns a young princeling who came to this country. He brought with him a famous jewel which he was to have reset for the lady he was going to marry, but unfortunately before that he made friends with a very pretty young lady. This pretty young lady did not care very much for the man, but she did care for his jewel—so much so that one day she disappeared with this historic possession which had belonged to his house for generations. So the poor young man, he is in a quandary, you see. Above all he cannot have a scandal. Impossible to go to the police. Therefore he comes to me, to Hercule Poirot. 'Recover for me,' he says, 'my historic ruby.' Eh bien, this young lady, she has a friend, and the friend, he has put through several very questionable transactions. He has been concerned with blackmail and he has been concerned with the sale of jewellery abroad. Always he has been very clever. He is suspected, yes, but nothing can be proved. It comes to my knowledge that this very clever gentleman, he is spending Christmas here in this house. It is important that the pretty young lady, once she has acquired the jewel, should disappear for a while from circulation, so that no pressure can be put upon her, no questions can be asked her. It is arranged, therefore, that she comes here to Kings Lacey, ostensibly as the sister of the clever gentleman—"

Sarah drew a sharp breath.

"Oh, no. Oh, no, not here! Not with me here!"

"But so it is," said Poirot. "And by a little manipulation I, too, become a guest here for Christmas. This young lady, she is supposed to have just come out of hospital. She is much better when she arrives here. But then comes the news that I, too, arrive, a detective—a well-known detective. At once she has what you call the windup. She hides the ruby in the first place she can think of, and then very quickly she has a relapse and takes to her bed again. She does not want that I should see her, for doubtless I have a photograph and I shall recognize her. It is very boring for her, yes, but she has to stay in her room and her brother, he brings her up the trays."

"And the ruby?" demanded Michael.

"I think," said Poirot, "that at the moment it is mentioned I arrive, the young lady was in the kitchen with the rest of you, all laughing and talking and stirring the Christmas puddings. The Christmas puddings are put into bowls and the young lady she hides the ruby, pressing it down into one of the pudding bowls. Not the one that we are going to have on Christmas Day. Oh no, that one she knows is in

　　　　　　　　　　　　　　The Missing Will & Other Stories

a special mould. She put it in the other one, the one that is destined to be eaten on New Year's Day. Before then she will be ready to leave, and when she leaves no doubt that Christmas pudding will go with her. But see how fate takes a hand. On the very morning of Christmas Day there is an accident. The Christmas pudding in its fancy mould is dropped on the stone floor and the mould is shattered to pieces. So what can be done? The good Mrs. Ross, she takes the other pudding and sends it in."

"Good lord," said Colin, "do you mean that on Christmas Day when Grandfather was eating his pudding that that was a real ruby he'd got in his mouth?"

"Precisely," said Poirot, "and you can imagine the emotions of Mr. Desmond Lee-Wortley when he saw that. Eh bien, what happens next? The ruby is passed round. I examine it and I manage unobtrusively to slip it in my pocket. In a careless way as though I were not interested. But one person at least observes what I have done. When I lie in bed that person searches my room. He searches me. He does not find the ruby. Why?"

"Because," said Michael breathlessly, "you had given it to Bridget. That's what you mean. And so that's why—but I don't understand quite—I mean—Look here, what did happen?"

Poirot smiled at him.

"Come now into the library," he said, "and look out of the window and I will show you something that may explain the mystery."

He led the way and they followed him.

"Consider once again," said Poirot, "the scene of the crime."

He pointed out of the window. A simultaneous gasp broke from the lips of all of them. There was no body lying on the snow, no trace of the tragedy seemed to remain except a mass of scuffled snow.

"It wasn't all a dream, was it?" said Colin faintly. "I—has someone taken the body away?"

"Ah," said Poirot. "You see? The Mystery of the Disappearing Body." He nodded his head and his eyes twinkled gently.

"Good lord," cried Michael. "M. Poirot, you are—you haven't—oh, look here, he's been having us on all this time!"

Poirot twinkled more than ever.

"It is true, my children, I also have had my little joke. I knew about your little plot, you see, and so I arranged a counterplot of my own. Ah, voilà Mademoiselle Bridget. None the worse, I hope, for your exposure in the snow? Never should I forgive myself if you attrapped une fluxion de poitrine."

Bridget had just come into the room. She was wearing a thick skirt and a woollen sweater. She was laughing.

"I sent a tisane to your room," said Poirot severely. "You have drunk it?"

"One sip was enough!" said Bridget. "I'm all right. Did I do it well, M. Poirot? Goodness, my arm hurts still after that tourniquet you made me put on it."

"You were splendid, my child," said Poirot. "Splendid. But see, all the others are still in the fog. Last night I went to Mademoiselle Bridget. I told her that I knew about your little complot and I asked her if she would act a part for me. She did it very cleverly. She made the footprints with a pair of Mr. Lee-Wortley's shoes."

Sarah said in a harsh voice:

"But what's the point of it all, M. Poirot? What's the point of sending Desmond off to fetch the police? They'll be very angry when they find out it's nothing but a hoax."

Poirot shook his head gently.

"But I do not think for one moment, Mademoiselle, that Mr. Lee-Wortley went to fetch the police," he said. "Murder is a thing in which Mr. Lee-Wortley does not want to be mixed up. He lost his nerve badly. All he could see was his chance to get the ruby. He snatched that, he pretended the telephone was out of order and he rushed off in a car on the pretence of fetching the police. I think myself it is the last you will see of him for some time. He has, I understand, his own ways of getting out of England. He has his own plane, has he not, Mademoiselle?"

Sarah nodded. "Yes," she said. "We were thinking of—" She stopped.

"He wanted you to elope with him that way, did he not? Eh bien, that is a very good way of smuggling a jewel out of the country. When you are eloping with a girl, and that fact is publicized, then you will not be suspected of also smuggling a historic jewel out of the country. Oh yes, that would have made a very good camouflage."

"I don't believe it," said Sarah. "I don't believe a word of it!"

"Then ask his sister," said Poirot, gently nodding his head over her shoulder. Sarah turned her head sharply.

A platinum blonde stood in the doorway. She wore a fur coat and was scowling. She was clearly in a furious temper.

"Sister my foot!" she said, with a short unpleasant laugh. "That swine's no brother of mine! So he's beaten it, has he, and left me to carry the can? The whole thing was his idea! He put me up to it! Said it was money for jam. They'd never prosecute because of the scandal. I could always threaten to say that Ali had given me his historic jewel. Des and I were to have shared the swag in Paris—and now the swine runs out on me! I'd like to murder him!" She switched abruptly. "The sooner I get out of here—Can someone telephone for a taxi?"

"A car is waiting at the front door to take you to the station, Mademoiselle," said Poirot.

"Think of everything, don't you?"

"Most things," said Poirot complacently.

But Poirot was not to get off so easily. When he returned to the dining room after assisting the spurious Miss Lee-Wortley into the waiting car, Colin was waiting for him.

There was a frown on his boyish face.

"But look here, M. Poirot. What about the ruby? Do you mean to say you've let him get away with it?"

Poirot's face fell. He twirled his moustaches. He seemed ill at ease.

"I shall recover it yet," he said weakly. "There are other ways. I shall still—"

"Well, I do think!" said Michael. "To let that swine get away with the ruby!"

Bridget was sharper.

"He's having us on again," she cried. "You are, aren't you, M. Poirot?"

"Shall we do a final conjuring trick, Mademoiselle? Feel in my left-hand pocket."

Bridget thrust her hand in. She drew it out again with a scream of triumph and held aloft a large ruby blinking in crimson splendour.

"You comprehend," explained Poirot, "the one that was clasped in your hand was a paste replica. I brought it from London in case it was possible to make a substitute. You understand? We do not want the scandal. Monsieur Desmond will try and dispose of that ruby in Paris or in Belgium or wherever it is that he has his contacts, and then it will be discovered that the stone is not real! What could be more excellent? All finishes happily. The scandal is avoided, my princeling receives his ruby back again, he returns to his country and makes a sober and we hope a happy marriage. All ends well."

"Except for me," murmured Sarah under her breath.

She spoke so low that no one heard her but Poirot. He shook his head gently.

"You are in error, Mademoiselle Sarah, in what you say there. You have gained experience. All experience is valuable. Ahead of you I prophesy there lies happiness."

"That's what you say," said Sarah.

"But look here, M. Poirot," Colin was frowning. "How did you know about the show we were going to put on for you?"

"It is my business to know things," said Hercule Poirot. He twirled his moustache.

"Yes, but I don't see how you could have managed it. Did someone split—did someone come and tell you?"

"No, no, not that."

"Then how? Tell us how?"

They all chorused, "Yes, tell us how."

"But no," Poirot protested. "But no. If I tell you how I deduced that, you will think nothing of it. It is like the conjurer who shows how his tricks are done!"

"Tell us, M. Poirot! Go on. Tell us, tell us!"

"You really wish that I should solve for you this last mystery?"

"Yes, go on. Tell us."

"Ah, I do not think I can. You will be so disappointed."

"Now, come on, M. Poirot, tell us. How did you know?"

"Well, you see, I was sitting in the library by the window in a chair after tea the other day and I was reposing myself. I had been asleep and when I awoke you were discussing your plans just outside the window close to me, and the window was open at the top."

"Is that all?" cried Colin, disgusted. "How simple!"

"Is it not?" said Hercule Poirot, smiling. "You see? You are disappointed!"

"Oh well," said Michael, "at any rate we know everything now."

"Do we?" murmured Hercule Poirot to himself. "I do not. I, whose business it is to know things."

He walked out into the hall, shaking his head a little. For perhaps the twentieth time he drew from his pocket a rather dirty piece of paper. "DON'T EAT NONE OF THE PLUM PUDDING. ONE AS WISHES YOU WELL."

Hercule Poirot shook his head reflectively. He who could explain everything could not explain this! Humiliating. Who had written it? Why had it been written? Until he found that out he would never know a moment's peace. Suddenly he came out of his reverie to be aware of a peculiar gasping noise. He looked sharply down. On the floor, busy with a dustpan and brush was a tow-headed creature in a flowered overall. She was staring at the paper in his hand with large round eyes.

"Oh sir," said this apparition. "Oh, sir. Please, sir."

"And who may you be, mon enfant?" inquired M. Poirot genially.

"Annie Bates, sir, please, sir. I come here to help Mrs. Ross. I didn't mean, sir, I didn't mean to—to do anything what I shouldn't do. I did mean it well, sir. For your good, I mean."

Enlightenment came to Poirot. He held out the dirty piece of paper.

"Did you write that, Annie?"

"I didn't mean any harm, sir. Really I didn't."

"Of course you didn't, Annie." He smiled at her. "But tell me about it. Why did you write this?"

"Well, it was them two, sir. Mr. Lee-Wortley and his sister. Not that she was his sister, I'm sure. None of us thought so! And she wasn't ill a bit. We could all tell that. We thought—we all thought—something queer was going on. I'll tell you straight, sir. I was in her bathroom taking in the clean towels, and I listened at the door. He was in her room and they were talking together. I heard what they said plain as plain. 'This detective,' he was saying. 'This fellow Poirot who's coming here. We've got to do something about it. We've got to get him out of the way as soon as possible.' And then he says to her in a nasty, sinister sort of way, lowering his voice, 'Where did you put it?' And she answered him, 'In the pudding.' Oh, sir, my heart gave such a leap I thought it would stop beating. I thought they meant to poison you in the Christmas pudding. I didn't know what to do! Mrs. Ross, she wouldn't listen to the likes of me. Then the idea came to me as I'd write you a warning. And I did and I put it on your pillow where you'd find it when you went to bed." Annie paused breathlessly.

Poirot surveyed her gravely for some minutes.

"You see too many sensational films, I think, Annie," he said at last, "or perhaps it is the television that affects you? But the important thing is that you have the good heart and a certain amount of ingenuity. When I return to London I will send you a present."

"Oh thank you, sir. Thank you very much, sir."

"What would you like, Annie, as a present?"

"Anything I like, sir? Could I have anything I like?"

"Within reason," said Hercule Poirot prudently, "yes."

"Oh sir, could I have a vanity box? A real posh slap-up vanity box like the one Mr. Lee-Wortley's sister, wot wasn't his sister, had?"

"Yes," said Poirot, "yes, I think that could be managed.

"It is interesting," he mused. "I was in a museum the other day observing some antiquities from Babylon or one of those places, thousands of years old—and among them were cosmetic boxes. The heart of woman does not change."

"Beg your pardon, sir?" said Annie.

"It is nothing," said Poirot. "I reflect. You shall have your vanity box, child."

"Oh thank you, sir. Oh thank you very much indeed, sir."

Annie departed ecstatically. Poirot looked after her, nodding his head in satisfaction.

"Ah," he said to himself. "And now—I go. There is nothing more to be done here."

A pair of arms slipped round his shoulders unexpectedly.

"If you will stand just under the mistletoe—" said Bridget.

Hercule Poirot enjoyed it. He enjoyed it very much. He said to himself that he had had a very good Christmas.

The original version of this story, "Christmas Adventure," can be found in the volume While the Light Lasts and Other Stories.

The Mystery of the Baghdad Chest

The words made a catchy headline, and I said as much to my friend, Hercule Poirot. I knew none of the parties. My interest was merely the dispassionate one of the man in the street. Poirot agreed.

"Yes, it has a flavour of the Oriental, of the mysterious. The chest may very well have been a sham Jacobean one from the Tottenham Court Road; none the less the reporter who thought of naming it the Baghdad Chest was happily inspired. The word 'mystery' is also thoughtfully placed in juxtaposition, though I understand there is very little mystery about the case."

"Exactly. It is all rather horrible and macabre, but it is not mysterious."

"Horrible and macabre," repeated Poirot thoughtfully.

"The whole idea is revolting," I said, rising to my feet and pacing up and down the room. "The murderer kills this man—his friend—shoves him into the chest, and half an hour later is dancing in that same room with the wife of his victim. Think! If she had imagined for one moment—"

"True," said Poirot thoughtfully. "That much-vaunted possession, a woman's intuition—it does not seem to have been working."

"The party seems to have gone off very merrily," I said with a slight shiver. "And all that time, as they danced and played poker, there was a dead man in the room with them. One could write a play about such an idea."

"It has been done," said Poirot. "But console yourself, Hastings," he added kindly. "Because a theme has been used once, there is no reason why it should not be used again. Compose your drama."

I had picked up the paper and was studying the rather blurred reproduction of a photograph.

"She must be a beautiful woman," I said slowly. "Even from this, one gets an idea."

Below the picture ran the inscription:

A recent portrait of Mrs. Clayton,

the wife of the murdered man

Poirot took the paper from me.

"Yes," he said. "She is beautiful. Doubtless she is of those born to trouble the souls of men."

He handed the paper back to me with a sigh.

"Dieu merci, I am not of an ardent temperament. It has saved me from many embarrassments. I am duly thankful."

I do not remember that we discussed the case further. Poirot displayed no special interest in it at the time. The facts were so clear, and there was so little ambiguity about them, that discussion seemed merely futile.

Mr. and Mrs. Clayton and Major Rich were friends of fairly longstanding. On the day in question, the tenth of March, the Claytons had accepted an invitation to spend the evening with Major Rich. At about seven thirty, however, Clayton explained to another friend, a Major Curtiss, with whom he was having a drink, that he had been unexpectedly called to Scotland and was leaving by the eight o'clock train.

"I'll just have time to drop in and explain to old Jack," went on Clayton. "Marguerita is going, of course. I'm sorry about it, but Jack will understand how it is."

Mr. Clayton was as good as his word. He arrived at Major Rich's rooms about twenty to eight. The major was out at the time, but his manservant, who knew Mr. Clayton well, suggested that he come in and wait. Mr. Clayton said that he had no time, but that he would come in and write a note. He added that he was on his way to catch a train.

The valet accordingly showed him into the sitting room.

About five minutes later Major Rich, who must have let himself in without the valet hearing him, opened the door of the sitting room, called his man and told him to go out and get some cigarettes. On his return the man brought them to his master, who was then alone in the sitting room. The man naturally concluded that Mr. Clayton had left.

The guests arrived shortly afterwards. They comprised Mrs. Clayton, Major Curtiss and a Mr. and Mrs. Spence. The evening was spent dancing to the phonograph and playing poker. The guests left shortly after midnight.

The following morning, on coming to do the sitting room, the valet was startled to find a deep stain discolouring the carpet below and in front of a piece of furniture which Major Rich had brought from the East and which was called the Baghdad Chest.

Instinctively the valet lifted the lid of the chest and was horrified to find inside the doubled-up body of a man who had been stabbed to the heart.

Terrified, the man ran out of the flat and fetched the nearest policeman. The dead man proved to be Mr. Clayton. The arrest of Major Rich followed very shortly afterward. The major's defence, it was understood, consisted of a sturdy denial of everything. He had not seen Mr. Clayton the preceding evening and the first he had heard of his going to Scotland had been from Mrs. Clayton.

Such were the bald facts of the case. Innuendoes and suggestions naturally abounded. The close friendship and intimacy of Major Rich and Mrs. Clayton were so stressed that only a fool could fail to read between the lines. The motive for the crime was plainly indicated.

Long experience has taught me to make allowance for baseless calumny. The motive suggested might, for all the evidence, be entirely nonexistent. Some quite other reason might have precipitated the issue. But one thing did stand out clearly—that Rich was the murderer.

As I say, the matter might have rested there, had it not happened that Poirot and I were due at a party given by Lady Chatterton that night.

Poirot, whilst bemoaning social engagements and declaring a passion for solitude, really enjoyed these affairs enormously. To be made a fuss of and treated as a lion suited him down to the ground.

On occasions he positively purred! I have seen him blandly receiving the most outrageous compliments as no more than his due, and uttering the most blatantly conceited remarks, such as I can hardly bear to set down.

Sometimes he would argue with me on the subject.

"But, my friend, I am not an Anglo-Saxon. Why should I play the hypocrite? Si, si, that is what you do, all of you. The airman who has made a difficult flight, the tennis champion—they look down their noses, they mutter inaudibly that 'it is nothing.' But do they really think that themselves? Not for a moment. They would admire the exploit in someone else. So, being reasonable men, they admire it in themselves. But their training prevents them from saying so. Me, I am not like that. The talents that I possess—I would salute them in another. As it happens, in my own particular line, there is no one to touch me. C'est dommage! As it is, I admit freely and without hypocrisy that I am a great man. I have the order, the method and the psychology in an unusual degree. I am, in fact, Hercule Poirot! Why should I turn red and stammer and mutter into my chin that really I am very stupid? It would not be true."

"There is certainly only one Hercule Poirot," I agreed—not without a spice of malice of which, fortunately, Poirot remained quite oblivious.

The Missing Will & Other Stories

Lady Chatterton was one of Poirot's most ardent admirers. Starting from the mysterious conduct of a Pekingese, he had unravelled a chain which led to a noted burglar and housebreaker. Lady Chatterton had been loud in his praises ever since.

To see Poirot at a party was a great sight. His faultless evening clothes, the exquisite set of his white tie, the exact symmetry of his hair parting, the sheen of pomade on his hair, and the tortured splendour of his famous moustaches—all combined to paint the perfect picture of an inveterate dandy. It was hard, at these moments, to take the little man seriously.

It was about half past eleven when Lady Chatterton, bearing down upon us, whisked Poirot neatly out of an admiring group, and carried him off—I need hardly say, with myself in tow.

"I want you to go into my little room upstairs," said Lady Chatterton rather breathlessly as soon as she was out of earshot of her other guests. "You know where it is, M. Poirot. You'll find someone there who needs your help very badly—and you will help her, I know. She's one of my dearest friends—so don't say no."

Energetically leading the way as she talked, Lady Chatterton flung open a door, exclaiming as she did so, "I've got him, Marguerita darling. And he'll do anything you want. You will help Mrs. Clayton, won't you, M. Poirot?"

And taking the answer for granted, she withdrew with the same energy that characterized all her movements.

Mrs. Clayton had been sitting in a chair by the window. She rose now and came toward us. Dressed in deep mourning, the dull black showed up her fair colouring. She was a singularly lovely woman, and there was about her a simple childlike candour which made her charm quite irresistible.

"Alice Chatterton is so kind," she said. "She arranged this. She said you would help me, M. Poirot. Of course I don't know whether you will or not—but I hope you will."

She had held out her hand and Poirot had taken it. He held it now for a moment or two while he stood scrutinizing her closely. There was nothing ill-bred in his manner of doing it. It was more the kind but searching look that a famous consultant gives a new patient as the latter is ushered into his presence.

"Are you sure, madame," he said at last, "that I can help you?"

"Alice says so."

"Yes, but I am asking you, madame."

A little flush rose to her cheeks.

"I don't know what you mean."

"What is it, madame, that you want me to do?"

"You—you—know who I am?" she asked.

"Assuredly."

"Then you can guess what it is I am asking you to do, M. Poirot—Captain Hastings"—I was gratified that she realized my identity—"Major Rich did not kill my husband."

"Why not?"

"I beg your pardon?"

Poirot smiled at her slight discomfiture.

"I said, 'Why not?' " he repeated.

"I'm not sure that I understand."

"Yet it is very simple. The police—the lawyers—they will all ask the same question: Why did Major Rich kill M. Clayton? I ask the opposite. I ask you, madame, why did Major Rich not kill Mr. Clayton."

"You mean—why I'm so sure? Well, but I know. I know Major Rich so well."

"You know Major Rich so well," repeated Poirot tonelessly.

The colour flamed into her cheeks.

"Yes, that's what they'll say—what they'll think! Oh, I know!"

"C'est vrai. That is what they will ask you about—how well you knew Major Rich. Perhaps you will speak the truth, perhaps you will lie. It is very necessary for a woman to lie, it is a good weapon. But there are three people, madame, to whom a woman should speak the truth. To her Father Confessor, to her hairdresser and to her private detective—if she trusts him. Do you trust me, madame?"

Marguerita Clayton drew a deep breath. "Yes," she said. "I do. I must," she added rather childishly.

"Then, how well do you know Major Rich?"

She looked at him for a moment in silence, then she raised her chin defiantly.

"I will answer your question. I loved Jack from the first moment I saw him—two years ago. Lately I think—I believe—he has come to love me. But he has never said so."

"Épatant!" said Poirot. "You have saved me a good quarter of an hour by coming to the point without beating the bush. You have the good sense. Now your husband—did he suspect your feelings?"

"I don't know," said Marguerita slowly. "I thought—lately—that he might. His manner has been different . . . But that may have been merely my fancy."

"Nobody else knew?"

"I do not think so."

"And—pardon me, madame—you did not love your husband?"

There were, I think, very few women who would have answered that question as simply as this woman did. They would have tried to explain their feelings.

Marguerita Clayton said quite simply: "No."

"Bien. Now we know where we are. According to you, madame, Major Rich did not kill your husband, but you realize that all the evidence points to his having done so. Are you aware, privately, of any flaw in that evidence?"

"No. I know nothing."

"When did your husband first inform you of his visit to Scotland?"

"Just after lunch. He said it was a bore, but he'd have to go. Something to do with land values, he said it was."

"And after that?"

"He went out—to his club, I think. I—I didn't see him again."

"Now as to Major Rich—what was his manner that evening? Just as usual?"

"Yes, I think so."

"You are not sure?"

Marguerita wrinkled her brows.

"He was—a little constrained. With me—not with the others. But I thought I knew why that was. You understand? I am sure the constraint or—or—absentmindedness perhaps describes it better—had nothing to do with Edward. He was surprised to hear that Edward had gone to Scotland, but not unduly so."

"And nothing else unusual occurs to you in connection with that evening?"

Marguerita thought.

"No, nothing whatever."

"You—noticed the chest?"

She shook her head with a little shiver.

"I don't even remember it—or what it was like. We played poker most of the evening."

"Who won?"

"Major Rich. I had very bad luck, and so did Major Curtiss. The Spences won a little, but Major Rich was the chief winner."

"The party broke up—when?"

"About half past twelve, I think. We all left together."

"Ah!"

Poirot remained silent, lost in thought.

"I wish I could be more helpful to you," said Mrs. Clayton. "I seem to be able to tell you so little."

"About the present—yes. What about the past, madame?"

"The past?"

"Yes. Have there not been incidents?"

She flushed.

"You mean that dreadful little man who shot himself. It wasn't my fault, M. Poirot. Indeed it wasn't."

"It was not precisely of that incident that I was thinking."

"That ridiculous duel? But Italians do fight duels. I was so thankful the man wasn't killed."

"It must have been a relief to you," agreed Poirot gravely.

She was looking at him doubtfully. He rose and took her hand in his.

"I shall not fight a duel for you, madame," he said. "But I will do what you have asked me. I will discover the truth. And let us hope that your instincts are correct—that the truth will help and not harm you."

Our first interview was with Major Curtiss. He was a man of about forty, of soldierly build, with very dark hair and a bronzed face. He had known the Claytons for some years and Major Rich also. He confirmed the press reports.

Clayton and he had had a drink together at the club just before half past seven, and Clayton had then announced his intention of looking in on Major Rich on his way to Euston.

"What was Mr. Clayton's manner? Was he depressed or cheerful?"

The major considered. He was a slow-spoken man.

"Seemed in fairly good spirits," he said at last.

"He said nothing about being on bad terms with Major Rich?"

"Good Lord, no. They were pals."

"He didn't object to—his wife's friendship with Major Rich?"

The major became very red in the face.

"You've been reading those damned newspapers, with their hints and lies. Of course he didn't object. Why, he said to me: 'Marguerita's going, of course.' "

"I see. Now during the evening—the manner of Major Rich—was that much as usual?"

"I didn't notice any difference."

"And madame? She, too, was as usual."

"Well," he reflected, "now I come to think of it, she was a bit quiet. You know, thoughtful and faraway."

"Who arrived first?"

"The Spences. They were there when I got there. As a matter of fact, I'd called round for Mrs. Clayton, but found she'd already started. So I got there a bit late."

"And how did you amuse yourselves? You danced? You played the cards?"

"A bit of both. Danced first of all."

"There were five of you?"

"Yes, but that's all right, because I don't dance. I put on the records and the others danced."

"Who danced most with whom?"

"Well, as a matter of fact the Spences like dancing together. They've got a sort of craze on it—fancy steps and all that."

                    The Missing Will & Other Stories

"So that Mrs. Clayton danced mostly with Major Rich?"

"That's about it."

"And then you played poker?"

"Yes."

"And when did you leave?"

"Oh, quite early. A little after midnight."

"Did you all leave together?"

"Yes. As a matter of fact, we shared a taxi, dropped Mrs. Clayton first, then me, and the Spences took it on to Kensington."

Our next visit was to Mr. and Mrs. Spence. Only Mrs. Spence was at home, but her account of the evening tallied with that of Major Curtiss except that she displayed a slight acidity concerning Major Rich's luck at cards.

Earlier in the morning Poirot had had a telephone conversation with Inspector Japp of Scotland Yard. As a result we arrived at Major Rich's rooms and found his manservant, Burgoyne, expecting us.

The valet's evidence was very precise and clear.

Mr. Clayton had arrived at twenty minutes to eight. Unluckily Major Rich had just that very minute gone out. Mr. Clayton had said that he couldn't wait, as he had to catch a train, but he would just scrawl a note. He accordingly went into the sitting room to do so. Burgoyne had not actually heard his master come in, as he was running the bath, and Major Rich, of course, let himself in with his own key. In his opinion it was about ten minutes later that Major Rich called him and sent him out for cigarettes. No, he had not gone into the sitting room. Major Rich had stood in the doorway. He had returned with the cigarettes five minutes later and on this occasion he had gone into the sitting room, which was then empty, save for his master, who was standing by the window smoking. His master had inquired if his bath were ready and on being told it was had proceeded to take it. He, Burgoyne, had not mentioned Mr. Clayton, as he assumed that his master had found Mr. Clayton there and let him out himself. His master's manner had been precisely the same as usual. He had taken his bath, changed, and shortly after, Mr. and Mrs. Spence had arrived, to be followed by Major Curtiss and Mrs. Clayton.

It had not occurred to him, Burgoyne explained, that Mr. Clayton might have left before his master's return. To do so, Mr. Clayton would have had to bang the front door behind him and that the valet was sure he would have heard.

Still in the same impersonal manner, Burgoyne proceeded to his finding of the body. For the first time my attention was directed to the fatal chest. It was a good-sized piece of furniture standing against the wall next to the phonograph cabinet. It was made of some dark wood and plentifully studded with brass nails. The lid opened simply enough. I looked in and shivered. Though well scrubbed, ominous stains remained.

Suddenly Poirot uttered an exclamation. "Those holes there—they are curious. One would say that they had been newly made."

The holes in question were at the back of the chest against the wall. There were three or four of them. They were about a quarter of an inch in diameter and certainly had the effect of having been freshly made.

Poirot bent down to examine them, looking inquiringly at the valet.

"It's certainly curious, sir. I don't remember ever seeing those holes in the past, though maybe I wouldn't notice them."

"It makes no matter," said Poirot.

Closing the lid of the chest, he stepped back into the room until he was standing with his back against the window. Then he suddenly asked a question.

"Tell me," he said. "When you brought the cigarettes into your master that night, was there not something out of place in the room?"

                                    The Missing Will & Other Stories

Burgoyne hesitated for a minute, then with some slight reluctance he replied, "It's odd your saying that, sir. Now you come to mention it, there was. That screen there that cuts off the draught from the bedroom door—it was moved a bit more to the left."

"Like this?"

Poirot darted nimbly forward and pulled at the screen. It was a handsome affair of painted leather. It already slightly obscured the view of the chest, and as Poirot adjusted it, it hid the chest altogether.

"That's right, sir," said the valet. "It was like that."

"And the next morning?"

"It was still like that. I remember. I moved it away and it was then I saw the stain. The carpet's gone to be cleaned, sir. That's why the boards are bare."

Poirot nodded.

"I see," he said. "I thank you."

He placed a crisp piece of paper in the valet's palm.

"Thank you, sir."

"Poirot," I said when we were out in the street, "that point about the screen—is that a point helpful to Rich?"

"It is a further point against him," said Poirot ruefully. "The screen hid the chest from the room. It also hid the stain on the carpet. Sooner or later the blood was bound to soak through the wood and stain the carpet. The screen would prevent discovery for the moment. Yes—but there is something there that I do not understand. The valet, Hastings, the valet."

"What about the valet? He seemed a most intelligent fellow."

"As you say, most intelligent. Is it credible, then, that Major Rich failed to realize that the valet would certainly discover the body in the morning? Immediately after the deed he had no time for anything—

granted. He shoves the body into the chest, pulls the screen in front of it and goes through the evening hoping for the best. But after the guests are gone? Surely, then is the time to dispose of the body."

"Perhaps he hoped the valet wouldn't notice the stain?"

"That, mon ami, is absurd. A stained carpet is the first thing a good servant would be bound to notice.

"And Major Rich, he goes to bed and snores there comfortably and does nothing at all about the matter. Very remarkable and interesting, that."

"Curtiss might have seen the stains when he was changing the records the night before?" I suggested.

"That is unlikely. The screen would throw a deep shadow just there, No, but I begin to see. Yes, dimly I begin to see."

"See what?" I asked eagerly.

"The possibilities, shall we say, of an alternative explanation. Our next visit may throw light on things."

Our next visit was to the doctor who had examined the body. His evidence was a mere recapitulation of what he had already given at the inquest. Deceased had been stabbed to the heart with a long thin knife something like a stiletto. The knife had been left in the wound. Death had been instantaneous. The knife was the property of Major Rich and usually lay on his writing table. There were no fingerprints on it, the doctor understood. It had been either wiped or held in a handkerchief. As regards time, any time between seven and nine seemed indicated.

"He could not, for instance, have been killed after midnight?" asked Poirot.

"No. That I can say. Ten o'clock at the outside—but seven thirty to eight seems clearly indicated."

"There is a second hypothesis possible," Poirot said when we were back home. "I wonder if you see it, Hastings. To me it is very plain, and I only need one point to clear up the matter for good and all."

"It's no good," I said. "I'm not there."

"But make an effort, Hastings. Make an effort."

"Very well," I said. "At seven-forty Clayton is alive and well. The last person to see him alive is Rich—"

"So we assume."

"Well, isn't it so?"

"You forget, mon ami, that Major Rich denies that. He states explicitly that Clayton had gone when he came in."

"But the valet says that he would have heard Clayton leave because of the bang of the door. And also, if Clayton had left, when did he return? He couldn't have returned after midnight because the doctor says positively that he was dead at least two hours before that. That only leaves one alternative."

"Yes, mon ami?" said Poirot.

"That in the five minutes Clayton was alone in the sitting room, someone else came in and killed him. But there we have the same objection. Only someone with a key could come in without the valet's knowing, and in the same way the murderer on leaving would have had to bang the door, and that again the valet would have heard."

"Exactly," said Poirot. "And therefore—"

"And therefore—nothing," I said. "I can see no other solution."

"It is a pity," murmured Poirot. "And it is really so exceedingly simple—as the clear blue eyes of Madame Clayton."

"You really believe—"

"I believe nothing—until I have got proof. One little proof will convince me."

He took up the telephone and called Japp at Scotland Yard.

Twenty minutes later we were standing before a little heap of assorted objects laid out on a table. They were the contents of the dead man's pockets.

There was a handkerchief, a handful of loose change, a pocketbook containing three pounds ten shillings, a couple of bills and a worn snapshot of Marguerita Clayton. There was also a pocketknife, a gold pencil and a cumbersome wooden tool.

It was on this latter that Poirot swooped. He unscrewed it and several small blades fell out.

"You see, Hastings, a gimlet and all the rest of it. Ah! it would be a matter of a very few minutes to bore a few holes in the chest with this."

"Those holes we saw?"

"Precisely."

"You mean it was Clayton who bored them himself?"

"Mais, oui—mais, oui! What did they suggest to you, those holes? They were not to see through, because they were at the back of the chest. What were they for, then? Clearly for air? But you do not make air holes for a dead body, so clearly they were not made by the murderer. They suggest one thing—and one thing only—that a man was going to hide in that chest. And at once, on that hypothesis, things become intelligible. Mr. Clayton is jealous of his wife and Rich. He plays the old, old trick of pretending to go away. He watches Rich go out, then he gains admission, is left alone to write a note, quickly bores those holes and hides inside the chest. His wife is coming there that night. Possibly Rich will put the others off, possibly she will remain after the others have gone, or pretend to go and return. Whatever it is, Clayton will know. Anything is preferable to the ghastly torment of suspicion he is enduring."

"Then you mean that Rich killed him after the others had gone? But the doctor said that was impossible."

"Exactly. So you see, Hastings, he must have been killed during the evening."

"But everyone was in the room!"

                                      The Missing Will & Other Stories

"Precisely," said Poirot gravely. "You see the beauty of that? 'Everyone was in the room.' What an alibi! What sang-froid—what nerve—what audacity!"

"I still don't understand."

"Who went behind that screen to wind up the phonograph and change the records? The phonograph and the chest were side by side, remember. The others are dancing—the phonograph is playing. And the man who does not dance lifts the lid of the chest and thrusts the knife he has just slipped into his sleeve deep into the body of the man who was hiding there."

"Impossible! The man would cry out."

"Not if he were drugged first?"

"Drugged?"

"Yes. Who did Clayton have a drink with at seven thirty? Ah! Now you see. Curtiss! Curtiss has inflamed Clayton's mind with suspicions against his wife and Rich. Curtiss suggests this plan—the visit to Scotland, the concealment in the chest, the final touch of moving the screen. Not so that Clayton can raise the lid a little and get relief—no, so that he, Curtiss, can raise that lid unobserved. The plan is Curtiss's, and observe the beauty of it, Hastings. If Rich had observed the screen was out of place and moved it back—well, no harm is done. He can make another plan. Clayton hides in the chest, the mild narcotic that Curtiss had administered takes effect. He sinks into unconsciousness. Curtiss lifts up the lid and strikes—and the phonograph goes on playing 'Walking My Baby Back Home.' "

I found my voice. "Why? But why?"

Poirot shrugged his shoulders.

"Why did a man shoot himself? Why did two Italians fight a duel? Curtiss is of a dark passionate temperament. He wanted Marguerita Clayton. With her husband and Rich out of the way, she would, or so he thought, turn to him."

He added musingly:

"These simple childlike women . . . they are very dangerous. But mon Dieu! what an artistic masterpiece! It goes to my heart to hang a man like that. I may be a genius myself, but I am capable of recognizing genius in other people. A perfect murder, mon ami. I, Hercule Poirot, say it to you. A perfect murder. Épatant!"